THE HEARTBREAK KID
Alison Kent

Harlequin Books

TORONTO • NEW YORK • LONDON
AMSTERDAM • PARIS • SYDNEY • HAMBURG
STOCKHOLM • ATHENS • TOKYO • MILAN
MADRID • WARSAW • BUDAPEST • AUCKLAND

In memory of two black dogs.

Thanks to the staff of Aldine Westfield Animal Hospital, Humble, Texas. Especially RVT Alison Abbott, for the tour. And Dr. Diane M. Fourie, DVM, for loving animals (even mine), and giving me a crash course in veterinary medicine.

Any mistakes are mine alone.

ISBN 0-373-25723-6

THE HEARTBREAK KID

Copyright © 1997 by Mica Kelch.

This edition published by arrangement with Harlequin Books S.A.

Printed in U.S.A.

"And you thought I was going to be easy," Sophie scoffed

She felt his gaze on her face as she studied the Scrabble board triumphantly. Another triple word score. "What are you looking at?"

"You'll take all the fun out of the game if you don't loosen up. C'mon. Enjoy the fire, the night." Tyler waggled both brows. "The company."

She rolled her eyes at yet another display of his ego. "Is that the type of sweet talk you used to draw your female opponents' attention away from the poker games?"

"They paid attention. They knew exactly when to hold 'em and when to fold 'em."

Sophie snorted, and stupidly spelled the word *girl* on the second *L* of *belly*. "If you marked the cards and the girls lost on purpose, what was the point of playing the game?"

Tyler took his time selecting his letters. Finally he lifted his long lashes to reveal eyes of glittering green.

"It's called foreplay, Sophie...darlin'."

The pause between those two words added an incredible intimacy. He ran his finger over the letters that spelled *belly*. Then he ran his finger over the letters that spelled *girl*. He took some letters and spelled the word *seduce* on top of another word.

Sophie felt her girl belly quicken and heat. "You can't put a word there."

"I can put anything anywhere I want to," he teased, then he crawled across the board and took her down to the floor.

Dear Reader,

February is the month for richly decadent chocolate, the perfumed scent of roses, and lacy valentines inscribed with romantic verse. It is also the month for lovers, which makes it the perfect month for you to fall in love along with Tyler Barnes and Sophie North.

Call Me, my first book for Harlequin Temptation, featured that gorgeous Texas rancher Gardner Barnes and the love of his life, Harley Golden. But somewhere between page 15, where Gardner's younger brother Tyler first appeared as a cocky eighteen-year-old, and page 206, where that cocky eighteen-year-old dispensed the wisdom of a man, Tyler became more than a supporting character. He became a heartbreaker.

Well, Tyler's all grown up now. Yessirree, all grown up. Those of you who've written and asked for his story won't have a bit of trouble recognizing the soul of that cocky eighteen-year-old, but ten years of maturity have made him a force to be reckoned with. He broke my heart (and that of my editor!), but Sophie North managed to hold hers together…for an hour or so….

Let Tyler break your heart, too. After all, this month is made for love. And lovers.

Please write and let me know if you fell in love.

Alison Kent

NEXT TIME her movie choices were limited to a testosterone fantasy or kickboxing beefcake, she'd be sure to stay home with her dog.

Shaking her head at the waste of a Sunday afternoon, Sophie North slammed the door of DayLine Construction's crew cab truck. She stood on tiptoe, gave a wave to her two co-workers sprawled across the back seat, then turned her gaze on the driver.

"What time tomorrow, Rico?" she asked.

"Six-thirty too early for you, *güerita?*" Rico's dare was cut off as zig-zagging lightning lit the northern sky and the thunder following rumbled through the metal frame of the truck.

Not about to be bested by the foul weather—or by her foreman's challenge—Sophie took up the gauntlet. "Make it six on the nose and the bacon and eggs are on me."

Rico put the truck back in gear. "Tired of your own cooking already?"

Before Sophie could respond, Dan leaned over the back seat and smiled. "I dunno, Rico. Judgin' by her size, it's not the cookin' she's tired of, but the eatin'."

"Maybe it's just the company," Sophie said, and scowled playfully.

"You're not gonna hafta worry about company if you

don't get a move on, girl. That wind comin' up's gonna blow you away." Dan nodded toward the approaching storm then sat back to an accompanying grunt from the third occupant of the truck.

J.D. spit a stream of tobacco juice into a Coke bottle and wiped his mouth on his sleeve. "We wouldn't have to be out in this weather if she'd stay in town. It's not like the motel ain't got the room."

"You know Sophie's rules, J.D." Rico held her gaze as he spoke. "She's a damn good electrician. Where she stays is her business. Not yours."

Sophie sent Rico a silent thanks. Working in what was traditionally a man's world brought resistance from time to time. But the fact that she insisted on separate quarters from her co-workers had never been a problem before J.D.

Too bad for him. No grumpy old man was going to drive her away from a job that was her best chance for finding her father.

She pulled her gaze from J.D. back to Rico and gave a farewell slap to the truck door. "I'll see you at six."

Rico winked his long dark lashes, put the big white truck in gear and drove off, leaving Sophie standing in a chalky cloud. Waving her hand in front of her face, she crossed the country road. Shells and gravel crunched beneath her boots. To the north, Mother Nature chimed in with more noisy promises.

The area was desperate for deliverance. The creeks were running low, the wells running lower. Even the cement mixers that poured the foundation at the DayLine site had stirred up enough dust to pave the road Sophie walked twice a day to the cabin she'd rented for the duration of this job.

Ford's Motel and Diner, the only lodging available in the small West Texas town of Brodie, had been happy to provide accommodations for the seven men of the DayLine crew. But Sophie didn't bunk with the boys.

Ever.

She'd grown up around construction sites and knew more than she wanted about the groupies who went for hard bodies in hard hats. Being mistaken for a construction camp follower wasn't going to happen. Being the daughter of one had been enough.

Rachel Ford, who waited tables in the family diner, had suggested Sophie talk to Sam Coltrain. Sam, who happened to be in Ford's at the time, offered her use of the cabin. The small bungalow had been a line shack until he'd converted it into quarters for his father before the elderly Coltrain passed on.

The road dust cleared and Sophie shook her head. Small towns. One person's business was another's—even when another was a complete stranger and would only be in the area for a couple of months.

Cowboy was waiting for her at the gate to the Coltrain place, sitting as motionless as a guard dog should. He wouldn't so much as wag his tail until she gave the word. He certainly wouldn't bark. But Sophie could tell he was fighting every canine instinct running in his blood.

"C'mere, big boy," she crooned, and then the black lab's paws were on her shoulders, his hind feet two-stepping all over her boots.

"I guess this means you've forgiven me." She

crouched to ruffle her hands over the dog's sleek coat. "I know you think you're human, but there are limits to what a human dog can do. Sitting through a two hour movie is one of them."

Tugging his ear playfully, she got to her feet, slapped her leg twice and headed down the drive. Cowboy fell into step beside her. A fierce blast of cold air plucked her T-shirt's thin threads and she lengthened her stride, pulling her jean jacket tighter.

Twenty feet later she saw the tire tracks.

Thirty seconds later she heard the gunshot.

She'd rigged the blast to startle trespassers and vagrants, to ward off hormonal teens who hadn't heard the local love nest was occupied. But, still, a shotgun was no toy...

Cowboy barked once and raced ahead, then waited for her to catch up. She did, sprinting now, pounding across the plank bridge spanning Little Creek. Within seconds she saw the cabin—and the red stepside pickup parked cockeyed to the front.

The truck was a flashy-looking thing; tinted windows, pin-striping, rims that looked to have been lifted from a spaceship. She wondered if she'd killed the owner.

Hurrying down the driver's side, she rounded the front of the vehicle and found her gunshot victim standing in front of the cabin's steps. He was quite alive. Quite unharmed, in fact. And quite intimidating.

It wasn't his size. Though tall, he was sleekly, subtly muscled. Black jeans encased strong legs and a braided leather belt circled his lean waist, the silver buckle riding flat on his lower belly.

It wasn't his appearance. If *he* was local stock, *she* was Snow White. From what she'd witnessed so far, the natives of Brodie, Texas, didn't come with this one's presence, his polish, his style.

No. It was the look in his eyes. The way they narrowed with each measured step she took toward him. The way his lashes, as sable dark and thick as they were, couldn't hide the glitter of green.

Fingers of cold air whipped madly at his longish hair, but it was cut to tousle. And the starched white fabric of his mother-of-pearl studded shirt snapped smartly in the strengthening wind.

He held the broom she kept on her porch in one large hand. The front door to the cabin stood open. He'd obviously used the first to push open the second—which just as obviously meant he'd discovered the alarm system she'd rigged up beneath her porch.

She came to a stop on the opposite side of the steps. Cowboy stopped beside her. The two-foot width of the two tiny stairs wasn't much in the way of distance or deterrent.

She was going to need one or the other.

"Is that your dog?" he finally asked into the whistling swirls of dust.

She nodded, digging her fingers into the ruff of Cowboy's neck, expecting an alert tension, finding him, instead, at ease. Interesting response, she thought, but didn't let go.

The man inclined his head. "I saw him up at the gate. Didn't recognize him as belonging to anyone in the county."

Sophie felt her brow lift. "You know all the dogs in the county?"

"I'm gettin' there," he said, and his grin pulled a dimple deep into one cheek.

That grin transformed him from intimidating stranger to intimidatingly attractive male. The grin wasn't flirtatious, or put on or planned. But it was who he was, she realized, and her stomach knotted in anticipation.

"That would make you, what? The local dog catcher?" She held Cowboy tighter. "That's it, isn't it? You're with the county animal control."

"In a manner of speaking. But you don't have anything to worry about—" he nodded toward Cowboy "—as long as he has all his shots."

"He does," Sophie said.

"Good. Otherwise I'd have to take him in and give 'em to him."

"Give them to him?" This was getting weirder by the minute.

"Now, don't be goin' all prickly on me. Livelihoods out here depend on healthy livestock, which is why I asked about his immunizations. I'm only doing my job."

"And what exactly is your job?"

He tossed the broom up onto the porch, dusted his hands together and propped them at his hips. "I'm Tyler Barnes. The local vet."

Tyler Barnes. The local vet. The local vet whose hospital she was building. The local vet with a smile to make a girl lose her balance. Not good when said girl spent her days running electrical wiring to fixtures twenty feet above the floor.

"No, don't tell me who you are," Tyler went on before she could think of a reply. "Let me guess. You look about the right age to be a friend of Lindy Coltrain's." When she frowned, he said, "Sam's daughter? Sam Coltrain? He owns this cabin?"

"I know who Sam is."

"Good. Thought I'd lost you for a minute." He moved his long fingers from his hips to his front pockets, leaned his backside against a porch post and took his sweet time. "I doubt Lindy would put up a friend this far from town, but Lucas is another matter."

Sophie lifted her blank gaze from Tyler's pockets to his face. What was it he'd said?

"Lucas? Lindy's brother?"

She moved her head noncommittally.

"Sam *has* been known to rent the place. So, I guess you could be passing through. 'Cept that nobody passes through Brodie, Texas." The corner of his mouth curled with all the subtlety of a big bad wolf.

It took a blast of cold wind to snap her to her senses. She huddled deep into her jacket, ignoring the temptation that came with that smile. "If you want to know who I am, why don't you just ask?"

"Who are you?"

"Sophie North."

"Well, Sophie North. You're obviously not from around these here parts," he said in a long, slow John Wayne drawl.

No doubt he'd've tipped back his Stetson if he'd been

wearing one. Sophie crossed her arms. "How can you be so sure?"

"First off, if you were, I'd know both you and your dog."

His mock arrogance had her compressing her lips. There was just something about a cowboy—even one who wasn't. This one might not make his living riding the range, but he had Wild, Wild West written all over him. And he definitely needed his cheeky attitude knocked down a peg.

A big fat raindrop obliged, smacking him between the eyes. Sophie managed not to laugh when he blinked and stepped back—a good thing since a second stinging splat hit her on the back of the head. Slapping her leg for Cowboy to come, she headed for the shelter of the porch.

Tyler followed, vaulting onto the warped board floor. "And secondly—" he picked up the conversation at the same time he picked up the broom and hooked the handle on the nail next to the door "—if you were, you wouldn't have call to rig up a shotgun under your porch."

Turning her way, he blinked slowly, his lids lazy, his expression expectant, and waited for her to reply. The rain began in earnest, the plop-plop of the first plump drops muffled by the pattering of the now steady shower. She turned her face to the diversion.

Why was it now that she had to notice how low the porch roof hung? How small the unenclosed space could be? How nice a man could smell wrapped in the fresh scent of cold sweet rain?

Her back to the wall, she crouched to rest her rear on

her heels. Cowboy lay at her feet. An envelope of mist hugged the cabin; she hugged herself, wrapping her arms close.

"I tripped the wire with the broom handle," he said, apparently quite content to carry the dialogue. "I'd seen the gun under the porch when I filled the dog's water bowl."

That explained what he'd been doing down there, but not the sense of expectation playing the notes of her body. She finally looked over. "Sam left me the gun for protection."

Tiny lines crinkled the corners of his eyes when he smiled. "He expected you to get some backlash from the kids, I guess."

Sophie frowned. "The kids?"

"Yeah. I'd imagine there's more than a couple of young lovers not too thrilled to find out you're living in Big O's. Not that you'd actually need a gun on account of—"

"Back up a minute." She really didn't want to ask, but, "Big O's?"

"Big Oscar. Oscar Coltrain. Sam's dad. The place was always known as Big O's. Once he passed on, the name sort of took on a new meaning, if you get my drift."

"I get it," she answered, wondering if she'd imagined the flush on Tyler's cheeks.

He took a couple of steps forward, braced his palm on a porch post and lifted his face to the cool breeze. The spray softly sprinkled the strands of his hair, dampened his skin and his crisp cotton shirt. Moisture beaded on his belt buckle and puddled on the fringed flaps of his black lace-up ropers.

Sophie swallowed hard and looked away.

"Like I was saying, even when they're rowdy they're a good bunch of kids. You call a place home all your life, you get to know your neighbors, the kind of folks they are, how they bring up their kids."

Sophie wouldn't know about any of that. The longest she'd called a place home was a year. Neighbors were hard to get to know when all you had in common was moving on. Still, most of the kids she'd known had done a good job raising themselves.

She knew she had.

"The folks living here work as hard on their families as they do on their spreads." She knew the instant he turned to face her. "You're as safe staying alone in this cabin as you are on this porch right now."

Safe? Now? Hardly. "Are you giving Big O's your stamp of approval?"

"It's been a while, but I've done my share of consumer testing." He reached up and touched the low-hanging porch roof, tracing a set of initials carved into the wood. "I think the tradition started a year or two before I knew about Big O's."

She had a feeling he knew more than anyone should about Big O's. "Tradition?"

"Yeah. Whoever got to Oscar's first on Saturday night left a flag on the gatepost. Sort of like a No Vacancy sign." Tyler grinned. "My Uncle Jud never did figure out what happened to all his bandannas."

All she could do was roll her eyes.

Tyler laughed and went on. "That was an ingenious alarm system, by the way. Don't think I'd ever realized rock salt made such a racket. You pick up that trick back home?"

"If you want to know where I'm from, why don't you ask?"

"Well, now, darlin', I might just. Long as you don't be goin' all prickly on me if I do."

He drew out the words in that sweet time drawl and walked toward her as he spoke. The front of his shirt was beyond damp. It stuck to his skin, revealing swirls of dark chest hair and the muscles beneath. The cords in his neck glistened, his spiky lashes swept down then up.

He made a gorgeous picture, this cocky cowboy with the heartbreaking grin. And she really had to stop looking.

"So, Sophie North. Where do you hail from?" he asked, stopping to lean against the porch post in her direct line of vision.

"No place in particular," she finally managed to reply.

"That makes it a tad difficult for folks to come a'callin'."

"I don't like folks to come a'callin'."

"Well, you certainly picked a good place to guarantee they won't."

Water bounced and ran off the hood of his truck. She glanced from the fancy pickup back to its fancy owner. "You did."

"I came about the dog."

"He's not much on socializing," Sophie said, scratching Cowboy's ears.

"His loss. I'm the best thing at socializing Brodie,

Texas has going right now. In fact, I'm on my way to see a little filly that can't get enough of me."

"Lucky you," Sophie commented, wondering whether the little filly was equine, or blond, red-haired or brunette.

He scratched his chin. "I don't know if I'd call it lucky. Last time I saw her she tried to take off my shoulder."

A blast of wind sent rain sheets skating across the porch. Sophie got to her feet, smoothed down her jeans and slapped her leg twice. "Cowboy. Inside."

The dog brushed by. Once in the cabin's main room, Sophie reached back to offer Tyler a sack or towel to use as an umbrella. But he'd already closed the door from the inside.

Crossing her arms over her chest, she gave him The Look. The one she pulled on new crew workers who had yet to learn Sophie's Rules. "I thought you had a filly to check on."

"I thought you invited me in."

The Look was a wasted effort. She recalled what she'd said, then, "Cowboy's my dog's name."

He propped his beautifully large hands at his waist. "Can't blame a guy for trying."

Well, no she couldn't. But she had more than a little say in his success. "Who does the filly belong to?"

Tyler strolled into the center of the cabin, filling her breathing room with the scent of soft rain and sun-dried cloth. "She's Sam's. Lindy invited me out for dinner, so I told Doc I'd save him the trip and chalk it up as my first house call."

Still leaning against the door, she arched a brow.

"Your first house call? So that means you're not really the local vet...yet."

His grin could move mountains. "I've been the local vet since I was about ten years old. It just took me another eighteen to make official."

Twenty-eight. Only two years her senior. Wind rattled the door and she moved away, closer to Tyler, then past him and on to the other side of the small kitchen table. "Well, I guess it'll be all right if you stay here until the storm blows over."

"Good, since I'm not going anywhere."

Rolling her eyes, she glanced around the main room and into the bedroom beyond. The comforter was pulled up over the sheets. And for once she'd actually folded her socks and nightshirt before tossing both onto the pillows.

"Why don't you sit there," she said, and pointed to the small brown-on-brown-plaid love seat. "I'll—" she waved her hand "—make some coffee or something." The kitchen was on the opposite wall. Good plan.

But apparently Tyler wasn't one for taking orders. He took one of the table's four ladder back chairs, spun it around and straddled it. The movement put him in her space again. "This seat's closer. You know, the better to hear you with."

"I can hear you fine from the love seat," Sophie said as she filled the kettle with water, set it on the stove and struck a match to light the burner.

"Not over that wind."

He was right about that. The ancient boards of the cabin creaked and groaned as the strengthening wind whistled through cracks of age. Cowboy didn't seem to mind at all. He'd passed out under the tiny table, right at Tyler's feet.

Her dog was taking the axiom of man's best friend too literally. Turning away, she shrugged out of her jean jacket and hooked the collar over the nail on the back door. "Does it do this a lot around here?"

"No. Just a couple of times during the fall. Sort of like Mother Nature's reminder that she could give us a hell of a winter if she wanted to. Give it a couple hours to wear off. Another hour for the road to drain and I'll be out of your way."

Three hours? Cooped up with a man possessing this one's earthy appeal? Who smelled like wind and sunshine? Whose smile had no doubt broken more than one heart? Right. Like she didn't know better than to court his kind of danger.

Tyler reached down to scratch Cowboy's ears. "I just hope it doesn't get worse, or go on long enough to throw off the hospital's completion."

Okay. Three hours. She could handle three hours. Scooping coffee into the drip pot, she snugged the drain top on tight. "Then maybe you should have taken the weather into consideration when you contracted to build this time of year."

He was quiet for a minute, staring at her dog. Then he blinked and smiled, as if a private thought had pleased him. "There're some things that just won't wait, you know? Like a dream?"

Slowly, Sophie resealed the coffee can and thought about dreams. Hers was to find the father who'd vanished when she was five, to experience the familial bond of belonging she'd missed in her younger years, to put what was left of her family together again.

She might have to wait a bit longer than Tyler, but she would see her dream fulfilled. Only then would her restlessness calm enough for her to return to school and finish her master's.

"Anyhow," Tyler continued, "I understand there's plenty of time built into the schedule. The building should be finished the week before Christmas. I don't want the construction workers to miss going home for the holidays."

He didn't know much about the DayLine crew, Sophie thought, returning the coffee can to the metal shelf in the corner. "I don't think bad weather delays are much of an issue at this point. The building's walled in. The remaining work is sheltered."

Tyler looked up. "How do you know so much about the building?"

Sophie shrugged. "I'm your electrician."

He straightened in the chair. "That's where I've seen your dog. At the construction site. But I don't remember seeing you."

"Most of my work's inside now. Besides—" She grabbed her hard hat from the kitchen counter and settled it on her head to hide her nape-length hair. "These unisex uniforms make it hard to tell one guy from another."

His gaze took in the white turtle shell of a hat with the boxy green "D/L" lettering before moving down. And down. Over her chin and the neckline of her T-shirt to her breasts.

Her shirt was thin, she knew. Thin enough without

her jacket to reveal the simple lines of her bra. His gaze slipped beneath her camouflage of plain sexless underwear and her pulse raced.

She wiped the sweat from her palms on her hips and Tyler's gaze followed the motion, drifting lower, to her belly, lower, lingering, drifting again. Finally, he lifted his lashes and wordlessly told her he didn't have a problem telling one guy from another.

She turned to stare at the water, willing it to boil, willing her heart to slow, her breathing to steady, the ache in her belly to subside.

"Is there a reason you're not stayin' at Ford's?" His voice reined in the silence riding wild through the room.

The kettle whistled. She removed the hard hat and reached for the distraction, pouring the water into the perforated top of the old-fashioned drip pot. "For one thing, ten hours a day is about all the togetherness I can handle."

"And reason number two?"

Sophie smiled. "I work with seven grown men who have convinced themselves that I can't take care of myself. They tend to be a bit...smothering. Of course, they don't have any trouble letting me mother them."

"I can see why they might be overprotective."

He was looking at her in that big bad wolf way again, a way she hadn't been looked at in a very long time.

Taking her mug from the drainer, a second from the cabinet, she carried both to the table and managed to bobble only one.

"Well, there is one who considers me a pain in the ass. But the others treat me like a daughter. Or a sister."

Tyler had his grin turned up full power and Sophie's stomach flip-flopped. "What are you smiling at?"

"Sophie and the seven construction workers. I guess that means the only position left for me to apply for is handsome prince...unless the position's already filled." He paused, offering her a chance to make up her mind.

For a moment she considered giving him an application, then decided his cocky attitude didn't deserve an answer. "Cream? Sugar?"

"Black is fine." After she poured her coffee and managed his without sloshing it onto his lap, he asked, "So, what's a girl like you—"

She shook her head, settling into the other chair. "Don't."

"You've heard that one before, huh?"

"At least twice on every job I've done."

"Been working construction long?"

"A couple of years." The work was easy. Most of her co-workers fun. The traveling she could handle since she'd never lived in one place long enough to grow roots. But there was one overriding reason she did what she did.

This profession was her best chance for finding her father.

"Seems an interesting career choice."

"For a woman you mean?" He lifted a brow at her comment and Sophie continued. "My father worked construction. I loved the sounds from the site." The rat-tat of the air tools. The grind and roar of machinery. The twang of steel high in the air. She sipped her coffee then cradled her mug between her palms.

She didn't tell him about the sound of arguing, or the

intensity of the fight that drove her father from her life, drove her mother into the arms of any available hard-hatted, hard body.

She swallowed another sip. Thunder shook the tiny cabin, the timpanilike vibration making Sophie too aware of the humming in her body. "You think this is going to last much longer?"

"Are we talking about the weather?"

"Just making conversation."

Tyler slouched back in the chair, laced his fingers over his belt buckle. "No, we're talking about the weather."

"I don't like complications." And she didn't. But it didn't stop her from enjoying the view. Or from asking, "Are you married?"

His lashes lowered. "Not married. Not engaged. Not even involved. But I intend to be before the end of next year. What are you laughing about?"

She couldn't help it. He was a wolf in wolf's clothing. "I'm trying to decide if that's optimism talking or just plain conceit."

"'Bout eighty part one, twenty the other. I'll let you pick the mix."

This time when the lightning cracked Sophie held on to the table. Tyler got to his feet, crossed the room and pushed aside the muslin curtain covering the small window above the kitchen sink. "Aw, hell."

"What?"

He turned back around and Sophie watched him study the cabin. He glanced into the tiny bedroom at the tiny single bed then back into the equally tiny main room at the tiny single love seat. She didn't like his resulting frown.

"Does that thing fold out?" he finally asked.

She looked at the love seat and back. "Why? What's wrong?"

He was slow to answer. Leaning back against the edge of the small countertop, he braced his hands at his sides. The heels of his palms curled over the lip of the sink.

The look he gave her was cocky cowboy and wicked wolf and full of the promise of sweet times.

"The bridge just washed into Little Creek. Looks like I'll be spending the night."

2

SOPHIE BARELY GAVE him time to get the words out before she spoke. "You can't stay here."

"I can't."

He hadn't asked it as a question, or stated it as a protest. He'd only repeated what she'd said.

She hardened her heart. He had to be aware of the awkwardness of her position. Besides, it wasn't as if he'd melt if he got wet. "No. You can't."

His frown deepened. It must've been her determined tone of voice or the haste with which she'd made her ruling. Whatever the cause, her intuition told her the unthinkable had happened.

She'd just rejected the heartbreak kid.

He managed to grin anyway. "Well, now, darlin', that's where you're wrong. It's gonna take more than that four-wheel drive out there to get me across Little Creek. And, as much as I hate to admit it, I'm a little rusty at walking on water."

His ego was entertainingly enormous. Refusing to crack even the tiniest smile, she considered her coffee and the situation. It wouldn't do to be trapped here alone with this man. This cowboy. This wolf in wolf's clothing.

Slowly, she got to her feet, careful to place her chair

between them. Flimsy as it was, she needed the barrier. "I don't suppose there's another way out of here."

"Well—" he narrowed one eye as if it helped him think "—Sam cut the road in far enough for Big Oscar to get his truck in and out. You go on past the cabin, you do it on horseback."

She curled her fingers around the chair's top rung. "I guess swimming the creek is impossible."

Glancing over his shoulder, he reached back and lifted one edge of the curtain. The rain was now a solid sheet of falling water. It was like looking through a roll of plastic wrap.

Sophie knew what he'd say before he said a word.

"You dip a toe in that gully washer out there, you're liable to end up a hundred miles downstream. Little Creek's a might bigger than its name right now."

"And there's not another bridge across?"

"Only the one at the road into Camelot. That's about five miles south of here."

"Camelot?"

"My brother's place. After that, the creek winds back deep into Gardner's land."

"Five miles isn't so far."

"Not if you're walking down the county highway. But to get to the Camelot bridge you'd have to follow the creek bank, and that red clay gumbo will suck you right down. Sam won't even be able to manage it with that plow he calls a grader until the surface water runs off."

"Well, how long—"

"Till I'm out of your hair? That's up to Mother Nature. First we gotta wait for the rain to let up and the ground to drain. Then we gotta wait for Sam to decide whether that ol' bridge is worth rebuilding or if he's gonna cut a new drive down past the bend in the creek."

Sophie grimaced. "Sounds like I'm going to be doing a lot of waiting."

"Hey, look on the bright side. You've got a nice place to wait in, nice company to wait with. I don't see why you'd even want to get out in that mess."

She didn't have the heart to tell him she wasn't going anywhere. She'd been trying to get rid of him. "So, exactly how long are we going to be stranded?"

He was looking her straight in the eye when he said, "I'd give it twenty-four hours."

"Twenty-four hours?" She took a step back. The chair's legs scraped across the wood floor. Cowboy scrambled up from under the table and headed to the hearth, giving her a "what did I do?" look over his shoulder as he passed.

"Might be closer to thirty-six. But don't worry." He crossed his arms over his chest, crossed one ankle over the other. "You won't even know I'm here."

She caught back a laugh, started to ask if he was serious then stopped when he pushed away from the sink and moved leisurely forward. His stride was long, slow and easy, and alive with the sweet-time attraction she wanted to avoid.

That one dimple in that one cheek deepened when he said, "Of course, if you're just itchin' to get to know me better, it would be downright unneighborly of me to say no."

Her breathing quickened. She saw his gaze measure

the rise and fall of her thin cotton shirt. "Why would I want to get to know you?"

"Well, let's see. I'm highly intelligent." He took one step, took another. The next brought him to the opposite side of her chair. "I have a great disposition. I'm good with kids."

Curling his hands beside hers on the chair back, he leaned forward. Her chin lifted. Her belly fluttered. She fixed her gaze on his spring green eyes and managed not to whimper or moan.

"And I'm so well trained I won't turn up my nose at anything you feed me."

Ah, food. The universal distraction. She ruffled a hand through her hair and glanced past him into the kitchen. "I haven't even thought about food. But now that you mention it—"

"Yeah. I'm starving, too." He straightened and let go of the chair, but didn't look away, confirming Sophie's fear that neither of them had been thinking about their stomachs.

"I'll get dinner started." She stepped around him, toward the kitchen, then stepped back behind the chair. She gestured with one hand. "It's just..."

"You worried about the sleeping arrangements?"

"Who said anything about sleeping?" This time the small laugh seemed to relieve her tension.

"Well, now, a good night's worth never hurt a working man. But it's not gonna matter much if you can't get across Little Creek in the morning."

"And rain or shine Rico will be at the gate out at the highway to pick me up at six. He won't know about the bridge. Rats. I need a phone." She glanced hopelessly around the cabin.

"I've got a radio in the truck. I'll see if I can raise Sam. He can tell Lindy I won't be along for dinner." He sat back down in his chair, squared an ankle on the opposite knee, unlaced and tugged off his boot. "I'll get him to give your foreman a call, too. What was his name?"

"Rico." She watched him reverse the process and tug at the second set of laces. "What are you doing?"

Boot number two hit the floor. He pulled off both socks, dropped them down into his boots and leaned forward to place his discarded footwear beside the front door.

Then, barefoot and quite at home, he stood and popped open the placket of mother-of-pearl snaps. "You got enough fuel to warm up this place?"

Sophie shivered. He hadn't answered her original question. She was sure of that. Just as she was sure she shouldn't be staring while he took off his clothes.

He draped his shirt over the back of the chair and turned her way. His shoulders blocked the light from the kitchen, casting him in a strong silhouette. She took a casual step to the side and released a small breath.

Mmm. Much better. The power she'd sensed earlier was evident now, with veins visible beneath the smooth skin of his arms, and lean strength defining his abdomen and chest.

The room's dim light rode the dips and swells of his masculine lines, delineating the grids of muscles shadowed with soft swirls of dark hair.

He was a powerful animal, the wolf she'd sensed. And feared.

"Sophie? Fuel?"

She nodded lamely, gestured toward the rear of the cabin and finally found her voice. "There's firewood under the tarp on the back porch. And Sam just had the butane tank filled."

"Then you might want to kick on the stove. What about blankets? Sam leave you any extras?" he asked, heading toward the front door.

Sophie followed, resisting the urge to bury her nose in the center of his back and inhale. "On top of the bureau in the bedroom."

"Good. Grab me one to wear when I get back."

No. She hadn't heard that right. "Wear? A blanket?"

"The way that rain's comin' down, my jeans are gonna be soaked before I make it to the truck." He opened the front door and gave her the biggest baddest wolfish grin so far. "This may be ranching country, but we still dress for dinner 'round these here parts."

Then he winked and was gone.

Sophie closed the front door and rested her forehead against the boards. The cabin walls receded, returning her space. The silence roared above the sounds of wind and rain. The air no longer buzzed electric but lay still and undisturbed.

Tyler had been in and out in less than thirty minutes and the room remembered.

From the corner of her eye she caught sight of his boots. Pivoting her head, she spied his shirt, closed her eyes and breathed deep. It was the scent of rain heated with male skin and she knew sleep would not come tonight or the next.

Life just wasn't fair.

Okay. She could do this. Spend the next two days cooped up in this cabin. This isolated cabin. This cold, isolated cabin—with a man whose smile warmed her from the inside out.

And she could do it without becoming her mother.

Unsnagging her hair from a chip in the door, she rubbed her hands vigorously over her arms as the drop in temperature settled into her bones. Briefly she considered checking on Tyler's progress, but seeing him dry and nearly naked had been enough excitement for her dormant hormones.

She needed to start dinner, but first she needed to start a fire. Tyler would be cold and wet. She didn't want him warming up and drying off at the stove where she'd be cooking. Figuring he wouldn't be outside long, she got started on the fire.

The wood Sam had left was seasoned and dry and it caught quickly. Cowboy paid no attention to her actions until he heard her at the stove banging pots and pans. Then he was sitting at attention and smiling for all of his doggie worth.

"Humph. A little attention and you're worthless as protection," she grumbled, checking the contents of the efficiency-size refrigerator. She decided Friday's potato soup would be more filling than the corn and tortilla she'd fixed yesterday and set it on the stove to reheat. She'd torn the top from a box of cornbread mix when she heard the knock.

Her head snapped up. *Tyler. The blanket. How could she have forgotten the blanket?* She knocked a raw egg to the floor in her mad dash for the bedroom. Snatching an old quilt from the top of the stack, she rushed back to answer the door.

More than Tyler's jeans had become soaked. His bare skin, his dark hair, his long and now spiky lashes, the tip of his nose. He grinned when a droplet fell, then shook his hair like a dog shook his bath. Sophie stepped back from the spray.

"Got a towel?" His teeth began to chatter, gooseflesh covered his arms.

Clutching the quilt, she returned through the bedroom and grabbed three of the folded towels from the rack in the alcove outside the tiny bathroom. Arms full, she retraced her steps, entering the main room, slowing as she came closer to the door that stood wide open.

His silhouette filled the rectangle of gray light. A curtain of rain hung behind him; the falling water roared like applause. Before he could take a bow, before she pulled up a chair, she shoved the linens into his hands. He handed back the quilt. She returned it.

He glanced from his left hand holding the towels to his right hand clenching the quilt. Then he looked at Sophie.

"You know, I've always wanted to be dried off by a blond pixie with bright green eyes. And now that I've got my hands full..." He let the sentence trail.

In your wildest dreams, she wanted to say. But since it was *her* dream wearing wet denim and holding the towels, she tightly compressed her lips, telling herself the shiver she felt was the cold.

She grabbed the quilt from his hands, hung it over the top of the open door and tossed the towels onto the seat of the chair she pulled over.

"There. Two free hands. I'll be in the kitchen." She headed in that direction. It wasn't a far enough walk. She could still hear Tyler laughing and she swore, above the rain and the wind and the creaky old cabin, she heard his zipper slide down.

Turning her back to the open door, she grabbed a fork and stirred the cornbread batter. Tyler moved into the room behind her, making "brrrr" noises and shivering. The fire hadn't yet started putting out much heat but she wasn't offering him use of the stove until she knew he was decent.

Decent. Tyler. What an oxymoron. Except *he* hadn't made an improper move.

The decency factor was all in her mind, where common sense and self-respect were having it out with lust. Separating the men she worked with—or worked for, in this case—from the men who were part of her personal life had never been a problem.

So why the trouble now? Why had she been ruffled by a physical attraction?

She knew the answer to both of her questions but refused to acknowledge his name.

"Did you have any luck on the radio?" she asked, stirring the pot of warming soup.

"I couldn't raise Sam but did manage to get through to Harley." He closed the door, the latch caught with a trigger-sharp click.

Sophie's heart jumped but her feet stayed on the ground. "Harley?"

"My sister-in-law." Keys and change clattered across the table. Cloth whispered, covering bare skin. Fire crackled and resin popped, warming the room and heating the scents in the air.

Sophie nudged Cowboy away from the back door and cracked it to let a breath of breeze into the kitchen. Filling the kettle to make iced tea, she asked, "What did she say?"

The wooden chair creaked as Tyler sat. "She called Ford's and explained our situation to your foreman. I couldn't hear what he said but his tone wasn't hard to interpret. Basically, he was, uh..." Tyler paused. "Glad to hear you're in such good hands."

Reaching for a box of tea bags, Sophie laughed. "Try again. If he was glad to hear anything it was the name of *your* next of kin. Rico's appointed himself my protector and he has the Latin temperament for the role."

"Yeah, that came across loud and clear," he said, sounding more amused than threatened. "But then Harley assured him of my high safety rating with the mothers of Brodie, Texas."

Safety rating?

The chair seat squeaked again. "I think the medical degree's what swayed him. Once he calmed down, he agreed I'd be handy to have around in case of an emergency."

"Like what? Rabies or distemper? The only emergency I can see happening is drowning," she said, glancing up toward the window.

"Speaking of drowning, it's a good thing you didn't take off on that five mile hike. Gardner barely got the Range Rover across Camelot's bridge before it went down into Little Creek. You and I aren't the only ones stranded."

Like that's supposed to make this easier? "So what did your sister-in-law say about the weather?"

"The squall line seems to have stalled. My predictions could be off."

Sophie turned off the burner beneath the soup. "You mean, it might not be thirty-six hours?"

"Could be forty-eight. Or longer."

"You are kidding."

"Do I look like I'm kidding?"

She finally turned. He'd pulled on his white socks and his white shirt. Though he'd fastened the snaps at his wrists, the shirt hung wide open. The tapered lines were cowboy cut and designed to fit a lean body—not a lean body already bundled up in a quilt.

The quilt was thin enough and worn enough that he'd been able to tie it around his rib cage. Still, it dipped in front, showing too much hair-dusted skin. And the edges barely managed to lap where they met along his thigh.

Judging by the way it fit Tyler's body, the quilt had been designed as a coverlet rather than a spread. Next time she'd be sure to check dimensions.

She glanced toward the fire, needing a brief distraction, getting one—and more. Tyler had pulled a chair in front of the fire, draped his black denim jeans over the back and a pair of black silk boxers over the seat.

This was really more than she wanted to know.

"I squeezed out most of the water. I'll put 'em back on soon as I can." He sounded apologetic, but not the least bit sorry. "I don't suppose you have a blow dryer?"

She slowly rolled her gaze his way. "You want to dry your hair?"

"No. My jeans." Her confusion must have shown because he added, "You'd be surprised at the survival skills I picked up in college."

Survival. Hmm. She doubted he'd devised any schemes more ingenious than the ones she'd used to stretch a dollar. Or the truth. "I have a blow dryer, but it's travel-size. Drying those jeans could take a while. Do you want to eat first?"

"Sounds good to me. Smells good to me." He pulled his chair to the table. "What're we having?"

She set out two crockery bowls, added two spoons and returned to the oven. "Soup."

"Soup?" Tyler glanced from the bowls to the spoons to the oven.

She plunked the hot skillet in the center of the table. "And cornbread."

"No meat and potatoes?"

"No meat, and the potatoes are in the soup." She hefted the kettle from the stove.

"That's it?"

"Nope." After filling two tumblers with ice and tea, she quickly sliced a tomato, a cucumber and a yellow bell pepper. "Vegetables."

"Raw vegetables?" His turned-up nose would've done a three-year-old proud.

A true brat if she'd ever seen one. She made a quick trip to the refrigerator, grabbed a bowl of shredded cheese. "Here. Sprinkle this in your soup."

He ladled soup into both their bowls and added

cheese to hers when she nodded. Then he took a bite. "Mmm. You always eat like this?"

"Do I always eat this well, you mean?"

"It is good," he admitted. "And, no, I meant... Spartan."

"Thanks. But I don't think of it as Spartan. I grew up eating soup from a can. Too often *straight* from the can." Scraping the back of her spoon over the lip of the bowl, she remembered the hard lessons of sink-or-swim independence. "I know a little about survival myself."

This time his smile was unnervingly tender. "Hey, I didn't do anything *but* survive. You turned your skills into something positive. Not everyone has what it takes to be a soup gourmet."

"It's no big deal. I travel a lot. Restaurants and fast food get old. Soup is filling and easy," she said, not wanting to remember any more.

"And M'm! M'm! Good! So what's for breakfast? Bacon and eggs? Ham and biscuits? Grits and gravy?"

Her hand stilled halfway to her mouth. She'd forgotten he'd be spending the night. *Yeah, right, she'd forgotten.* She took the bite, swallowed, then said, "Oatmeal and bananas."

"Oatmeal and bananas?"

Sophie glanced at the bowl of fruit on the countertop. "I'll save the apples for the morning after. I'm afraid the bananas won't last another day."

She looked back at Tyler, but judging by the pained look on his face he seemed to be struggling with the concept.

"Tyler, it's not that difficult. I eat simply. I dress simply. I'm on the road. I work long hours. I don't have time to cook." She pointed at him with her spoon. "Besides, you said you wouldn't turn up your nose at anything I fed you."

"And as long as it's not tuna or macaroni and cheese I'll be glad to keep my word."

"More college survival skills?"

Spoon in his mouth, he nodded then swallowed. "Yeah. Gardner put me through school, but he also put me on a monthly allowance. The first month I blew it in a week."

"Uh-oh."

"Uh-oh is right. That was the one and only time big brother bailed me out. When I did it again the next month, he *loaned* me the money. I had to work it off at the ranch over Christmas break. I didn't do it again after that."

"I guess this is where the tuna and macaroni and cheese come in."

"You got it."

"Well, if you ever get in another financial bind, remember the soup. It comes in more varieties." She spooned up her last bite.

"Thanks, but right now going hungry is the least of my worries. Every Brodie County mother I know is cooking up a storm of chicken-fried steak and cream gravy, trying to convince me they've taught their daughters everything they need to know to make the perfect veterinarian's wife."

He leaned his chair back and patted his belly. "I'm gonna weigh a ton this time next year."

His heartbreaking grin weighed a ton. So did the

urge to lower her gaze from his face. "Won't you find it tough to give up all that attention and settle down?"

"Hey, I plan to settle down. I never said anything about giving up the attention. Why should I?"

For a moment she couldn't move, then she began stacking the empty dishes. "How do you think your wife will feel about all this attention you don't plan to give up?"

He looked at her as though she'd lost her mind. "Since she's the one I plan on getting it from, she damn well better be willing."

Oh. Well. That made it a bit easier to finish gathering the dishes without breaking one or two.

"Shoot. Why do you think I'm sacrificing my fighting weight for all that home cooking?" Leaning his forearms on the table, he fingered another pepper strip, grabbed it up and chomped down.

Sophie arched a brow. "I assumed you were judging the contestants' culinary skills."

"It's the mothers impressing me with the culinary skills. I'm judging the contestants on that willing part."

That sweet-times look in his eye really did make the word "willing" easy to understand. Lips compressed, she got to her feet and took the dishes to the sink.

"You have a good point, though," he said, carrying on without her.

She tried to look vaguely interested when what she really wanted to do was prick up her ears. "Oh?"

"I'm going about this all wrong, aren't I? I'm working it like a business deal instead of just letting it happen."

Not only that, she wanted to say, *you're judging them, sampling them, calling them willing contestants.* But it wasn't any of her business, so instead she said, "I don't know. Guess that depends on how important home cooking is to the merger."

The big bad wolf was back. "Definitely not as important as that willing part."

This conversation had strayed where she didn't want to go. Looking from Tyler back to the sink, she said, "Why don't I go get that hair dryer?"

She cleaned up the dishes while Tyler dried his jeans. Her head had begun to ache from the ceaseless pounding of the rain on the cabin's roof. Or maybe it was from the stress of the close quarters, the conversation and the night to come.

She needed a breath of air that didn't smell like Tyler. And Cowboy was due for a trip outside. She dried her hands and opened the back door. Grabbing her jean jacket off the door hook, she slapped her leg for Cowboy to come.

When she turned back to see what was keeping him, he looked at her as if she'd lost her mind. "You and Tyler been practicing that look behind my back?" she murmured for his ears only.

The dog whimpered.

"Sorry, bud. It's either out in the rain or under the cabin. Take your pick."

Cowboy placed two tentative paws on the top step, looked at Sophie a final pitiful time then jumped down and disappeared beneath the cabin. Though the air was more cold than refreshing, Sophie found a stable stack of firewood, parked her butt and took a deep, cleansing breath. Thunder rolled overhead, a rumbling bass beat to the relentless rhythm of the rain.

Leaning her elbows on her knees, she stared sightlessly into the black liquid and thought of all the night skies she'd seen from tenement fire escapes or tarred rooftops. Each city she'd lived in brought a subtle shift to the constellations' position and brilliance.

Yet the stars always had a home in the sky, while she had belonged nowhere—and, quite frankly, to no one.

Her father had disappeared when she was five and the only thing she'd blamed him for later was not taking her along. He'd left Sophie to live with a mother whose sole pastime, pleasure, and purpose in life was notching her bedpost with the man of the month.

Sophie had fed herself, clothed herself and given every city's social workers the right answers. Living with her mother was better than the alternative of placement in a foster home where her father would be unable to find her.

Or so her childish mind had determined. She'd been too young to know about custodial rights or a parent who moved a child like a pawn. And she hadn't learned the truth until after her mother's death.

When sorting through her mother's belongings, Sophie had found six painstakingly, hand-scrawled letters her father had written. No envelopes. No return address. No clue in the body as to where he was, how to find him, why he'd stopped writing.

Or why her mother had saved them.

That one puzzle would never be solved, but other answers were out there, waiting to be found with her father.

He'd written. Every year on her birthday, he'd written. He'd wanted her, had begged her mother to let him give Sophie the life she deserved. He'd offered permanence, a life instead of an existence.

Her mother had never told her. Never. Sophie never had a clue. And even as a mature adult of twenty-six, she'd found it hard not to indulge her anger, to cap off a lifetime of resentment with hatred.

But at five, she couldn't figure out what she'd done wrong, or what she needed to do right. Later, she'd thought her father must've feared she'd become too much like her mother. Too eager for fun and excitement. Too recklessly impulsive. Too intent on self-satisfaction to think of others.

It had been easy, as a child, to lock away her feelings; harder, as an adult, to remember where she'd put them.

Cowboy jumped back onto the porch and settled at Sophie's feet. She rubbed her hand over his damp fur. "Mmm. Nice doggie perfume, bud." But not quite what she'd had in mind as an alternative to smelling Tyler.

Tyler. She'd come outside to shed the man, but he clung to her skin like mist from the rain. Why, when her response to him was nothing but lust at first sight? And when she knew firsthand that passion destroyed perspective and common sense.

From the time she'd understood what went on between men and women, she'd known her mother's string of lovers was not representative of anything society considered normal.

She'd known that relationships needed more than a physical basis. First, a foundation of friendship. Then respect and care and concern. And finally a warm, cozy and safe attraction.

Not a flash-fire lust that consumed what it touched.

She knew all this. She kept the credo in the back of her mind. That's why all this crazy desire she felt for Tyler was…crazy.

And why now that she'd talked it over with herself she could return inside and make it through the night without becoming her mother.

3

WHEN SOPHIE WALKED back inside, a blast of heat hit her in the face. Tyler had draped his jeans over the oven's open door. The hair dryer was lying in the center of the kitchen table. It was not exactly what she'd expected to find.

She closed her eyes, counted to ten and breathed deeply of damp denim and lightly smoked air. Cowboy lumbered by on his way to the hearth, knocking her off balance and brushing beads of moisture from his coat onto the leg of her jeans.

"Worthless dog," she said, catching herself on the edge of the sink. Once steadied, she glanced up to see that Tyler had been busy with more than creating methods for drying his clothes.

He'd turned the love seat to face the fire. He'd also set the room's only lamp in the corner on the floor, giving himself access to the footlocker that had been the lamp's table.

And now he was digging through the footlocker, wearing nothing but his socks, his shirt and his black silk boxers.

Ignoring the rush of heat to her face, she asked, "What happened to blow drying your jeans?"

He glanced around, his expression too welcoming for

the length of time she'd been gone. "Hey, you're back. I wondered where you'd gotten to."

"I took Cowboy out." She moved the five short steps from the sink to the table and hooked the dryer with her finger. "Give up so soon?"

"I didn't give up. The hair dryer did. I think it overheated. At least I got my shorts dry." He stood to model them for her, holding the legs out like black bat wings.

He'd buttoned his shirt and the tails flapped long enough to cover vital areas. The shorts themselves hit him mid-thigh. They were as decent as any pair of cutoffs; more decent than most bathing trunks.

But it was just the fact that they were underwear that Sophie found hard to overlook.

Tyler turned back to his digging project. "How 'bout a game? It'll have to be checkers or Scrabble. There used to be a Monopoly set but this is all I could find." He held up a crumpled gold five hundred dollar bill.

Sophie considered his suggestion. A game would be good. To pass the time. To keep minds absorbed and the mood amicable. To keep her awake and fully clothed when her bed and red flannel nightshirt beckoned.

It was going to be a long two days.

She shrugged off her jacket, tossed it onto the table, then walked into the living area, stopping on the back side of the love seat. "How did you know about the games?"

"I've spent some time here, remember?" A wicked hint of the wolf curled his lip when he picked up a deck of cards and pointed out several insignificant markings.

"And I played many a winning hand of poker with this deck."

Sophie took the cards from his hand and studied the red and white backs. "That doesn't seem exactly fair. Marking the cards."

"*Au contraire.* All's fair in love and war. Especially when you're seventeen and your date suggests a game of strip poker."

Wolf, nothing. This one was a crafty fox. She returned the deck and added a touch of censure to the upward tilt of her nose. "Your opponents never caught on?"

Taking the cards, Tyler shrugged. The corner of his mouth pulled further upward and that one dimple appeared in his cheek. "I don't know if they did or not. They were too busy trying to lose."

"How modest of you to notice."

"The ego runs in the family. You ought to meet my brother. No, you ought to meet any one of his sons. They're three, six and nine and full of Barnes blood." He shuffled the cards hand to hand, gave her a smoky look from beneath his long lashes. His grin had reached outrageous proportions. "I guess poker's out of the question?"

"So is blackjack, gin rummy, hearts, old maid or any game involving those cards." She'd already handicapped him by allowing him to play in his underwear.

He tossed the deck over his shoulder; the cards scattered in the bottom of the footlocker. "Then Scrabble it is—as soon as we decide on the stakes."

Considering the deck of marked cards, Sophie had the feeling any stakes Tyler named would lean in his favor. And she was not about to give the upper hand to a man in his state of dress. Uh, undress.

"Why don't we play for fun? And I don't mean your strip poker kind of fun," she added before he had a chance to turn the conversation in that direction again.

How he managed to look disappointed and guilty at the same time she didn't know. She *did* know his vulnerable-puppy-dog look was going to get her in big trouble.

At the moment, however, trouble was a rear end covered in black silk boxers. Tyler had turned and now stood leaning over the footlocker, his shirttail hiked high.

Sophie spun and walked in the opposite direction. A long two days, nothing. The next forty-eight hours loomed like an eternity. What was it about Tyler Barnes? Why now, when she was stranded in this tiny cabin in the middle of God's country, did she have to feel this strong physical attraction for a man?

By the time she'd rounded the love seat, she'd talked herself back into control. Tyler was standing upright with his shirttail back in place. Now, as long as they both remained controlled and upright, forty-eight hours would be no problem.

Tossing the board game onto the cushions of the love seat, he grabbed up his discarded quilt and spread it on the floor. "I've decided on the ante."

This should be good. "And?"

"The winner gets to sleep in the bed. The loser gets stuck with the love seat."

"Tyler, I don't mind sleeping on the love seat. You

take the bed." He was taller, broader, and she could always wash his smell out of the sheets later.

Hands at his black silk hips, he cocked one brow. "You give up so easy, a guy could get the wrong idea."

Easy? He thought she was going to be easy? Not in this lifetime. "Just set up the board, Dr. Barnes. Let's see what fancy words they taught you in college."

He chuckled and reached for the game. "There's only one thing I love more than a woman who's easy."

"What's that?"

"A woman who makes me work for it," he said, and she couldn't even think to reply.

Cowboy reluctantly gave up his space near the fire and trotted off to the kitchen. Tyler arranged their playing area on the floor in front of the hearth. The firelight worked magic, highlighting strands of mahogany in the darker brown of his hair, casting shadows of his lashes down his cheeks, bathing the resilient skin of his throat in golden tones.

Sophie couldn't help but feel this one hadn't had to work for much of the female attention he'd received in his life. He was a West Texas fantasy waiting to be unwrapped—even if at the moment he was a little too unwrapped for her liking.

Once he'd settled cross-legged on one side of the game, she stepped back into the bedroom, grabbed up a faded floral blanket and tossed it in his lap. "I wouldn't want you to catch cold or anything."

He fingered the pink satin binding and raised his cocky gaze. "I won't need this once the competition heats up."

Sophie sighed. Sooner or later she'd grow inured to his overly confident grin. Or maybe not.

"Keep it." She sat across from Tyler, her back to the love seat, her legs outstretched, her soles flush against the stone hearth. "We'll use the heat from the competition to dry your jeans."

Tyler laughed then. The sound was huge and healthy and playful, and one-hundred-percent heartbreakingly male. Sophie crossed her ankles, curled her toes in her boots and fought the rising image of what lay underneath the faded floral blanket.

With much battling over the wooden squares, they both picked their letters then drew for position. Sophie won and went first. She studied her selection then laid six letters down to spell *wiring*.

Tyler frowned. "That was close. One more letter and I'd've had to demand a rematch. Or at least the best two out of three."

"And you thought I was going to be easy." Thank goodness she'd proved him wrong. And proved herself right. She pulled out six more letters then added her points. "Rats. I didn't get a pencil or anything to keep score on."

"Hang on." Leaning back, Tyler plucked a pencil stub out of the footlocker and handed her the crumpled gold five hundred dollar bill. Then he spelled *lips* using the first *l* of her word.

She felt his gaze on her face as she studied the board and tallied their scores. Felt it still while she recorded the totals on the scrap of gold paper held against her thigh. Felt it even when she'd finished and had no reason not to look up.

So, she did. "What are you looking at?"

"You know, Sophie. When you get serious or, like now, when you're concentrating on what you're doing, you smash your lips together so tight it looks like you'd need a cattle prod to pry them apart."

"I do not," she said, deliberately relaxing her mouth. "And if you're trying to distract me it's not going to work." She showed him the numbers. "I'm already ahead by four points."

"And already as tight as a barbed wire fence. You're going to take all the fun out of game if you don't loosen up. C'mon. Enjoy the fire, the night." He wiggled both brows. "The company."

She rolled her eyes at yet another display of his ego. "Is that the type of sweet talk you used to draw your female opponents' attention away from the poker games?"

"They paid attention. They knew exactly when to hold 'em and when to fold 'em."

Sophie snorted and spelled *siren*. "If you marked the cards and they lost on purpose, what was the point of playing the game?"

Tyler took his time selecting his letters. Took even longer answering her question. Finally he lifted his long lashes to reveal eyes of glittering green.

"It's called foreplay, Sophie, darlin'."

It was hard to respond with no heartbeat, no pulse, no intake of breath. "Why bother if a trip to this cabin had an obvious result?"

"Why bother?" He didn't try to hide his surprise. He merely shook his head and stretched out on his side, stirred the letters in the box top, moved his index finger in a maddeningly slow figure eight, around and back, around and back. "Don't you know anticipation makes the world go 'round?"

She set the pencil and paper aside and, feeling every one of her stiff, mechanical movements, got to her knees to punch up the fire. Sparks flew and smoke plumed and she welcomed the warmth on her face. The flush from the fire was acceptable, the heat of innuendo was not.

Nothing about this night was proceeding as planned, but then nothing in her experience had prepared her for Tyler Barnes. He was everything a man could be, everything she'd known she had the strength to resist.

She'd been wrong. He'd rocked her world and she wasn't sure how to slow the momentum.

Because she had to, she sat back and resumed both her scorekeeping position and her determination to keep things light. The first words out of Tyler's mouth blew her dwindling resolve.

"You're doing that thing with your lips again."

She slowly lifted her gaze, ready to recite Sophie's Rules, but the intent in his eyes turned her to warm, willing mush.

He reached across and, using the pad of his thumb, separated the seam of her tightly held lips. "But I was wrong. It's not going to take a cattle prod after all."

Sophie didn't dare move, didn't dare lick her lips. He'd left a hint of his taste on her mouth. Resistance followed the wild need to swallow. She didn't want to know his flavor, to remember, to want it again.

"Your turn."

Fighting the swelling in her throat, in her breasts, but

mostly in her heart, she looked down to the board to see he'd spelled his next word. *Neck*.

Using his *C* to spell *credit*, she looked back to the fire. He'd touched her lips. Her lips, for goodness' sake, and she'd heated up as if the flames were licking her skin instead of the logs burning red hot in the grate.

The response was unnerving, unsettling, and worlds removed from what she'd felt during the only serious romances she'd had in her life. Both relationships had been safe and had fizzled without fulfillment. But that helpless sense of failure was nothing compared to the frustration tearing at her now.

The physical response to Tyler burning through her body was erotic, carnal and empowering. It made it impossible to deny, and harder to admit, that her mother's passionate nature was also her own.

"Hey, scorekeeper. You're getting behind."

The pencil shook, but she managed to record the scores. Then, since it was her turn, she spelled *edit*. And Tyler slipped an *E* and an *A* between the ending *T*'s of her last two words.

She could only blink. This time he'd stepped over the line.

Slowly, he shook his head. "Now, don't be goin' all prickly on me. I was a rancher long before I was a vet. The word *teat*'s about as asexual as you can get."

He was right. Her obviously warped mind was making too much of it—a reaction easy enough to understand. The earlier talk about foreplay had her rattled.

Be honest, Sophie. It's the earlier demonstration *of foreplay that has you rattled.*

Using the eraser end of the stubby pencil, and using

an incredible amount of forced calm, she pointed to his words on the board. "You seem overly obsessed with body parts tonight."

He gave a casual, one-shouldered shrug. "Some body parts deserve obsessing over."

"You mean, one pair of lips isn't as good as another?"

"Hell, no. There are some I want to kiss and some I don't."

Ah, a discriminating wolf. She hadn't been witness to much discrimination in her life. It made her curious, dangerously so. "What is your criteria for separating..."

"The lips I want to kiss from the ones I don't?"

She nodded, knowing by the flush rising to her face that it was time to punch the fire again.

"They have to be giving. Accepting. And soft." He repeated his earlier gesture and rubbed her willingly parted lips with his thumb. And, when he moved his hand away, firelight glinted off the dampness she'd left on his skin.

"Most of all, they have to taste sweet," he said, and pressed the moisture to his mouth.

Sophie looked down at the board because she didn't trust herself to look at his thumb. Or his mouth. Or his eyes. With a pit of heat in her belly, she spelled her next word. *Barn*. He spelled his. *Rib*. She tallied the scores, her gaze drifting back to the second body part word he'd constructed.

She touched her pencil tip to the *N*, the *E*, the *C* and the *K* before bravely—or was it foolishly?—glancing up. "How do you feel about..."

"Necks?" he finished for her. Raising up to his hip, he braced his weight on an elbow, pulled up one knee and tugged at the pink satin binding of the blanket that had almost slipped to the floor. "Necks are as individual as their owners. For a long time my favorite was dusted with red freckles. Then I liked one that was long and soft as new down.

"But I also like feminine strength. Especially when it's been touched by the sun."

She waited for him to caress the sun-touched strength of her feminine neck, to pull her closer and test the sweet, giving softness he'd found on her lips. But he turned his gaze to the board.

"Your turn."

She looked down and found the presence of mind to spell *ewe*.

"Another livestock word?"

Exhaling slowly, she said, "Yeah, a livestock word that just put me way ahead with a double word score."

"Then let's see if I can make use of this triple word square over here. I don't intend to give up my mattress rights so easily."

And while she watched, while the words *foreplay* and *anticipation* ran through her mind, while the fire warmed her face and her body hummed with expectant energy, Tyler spelled the word *belly*.

She barely consoled herself with the fact that he only got the double word score. Belly was a body part she didn't want to hear him talk about—especially with the ache building low and deep in hers.

Turning her full attention back to the game, she stupidly spelled the word *girl* on *belly*'s second *L*.

She knew he was waiting, watched his eyes drift from hers to the words they'd spelled and back. She swallowed hard, took in more of his taste and decided that anticipation frightened her more than her mother's blood.

"Sophie. Darlin'."

The pause between those two words added an incredible intimacy. He ran his finger over the letters that spelled *belly*. Then he ran his finger over the letters that spelled *girl*. "Isn't there something you want to ask me?"

Sophie felt her girl belly quicken and heat. She licked her lips, parted them and wisely answered, "Did you know it's your turn?"

"That wasn't what I was waiting to hear," he said, and slowly, one wooden letter at a time, used the final *E* of her word *ewe* and built the word *seduce*.

"No two bellies are alike. Some lay flat, afraid to grow up. Others are gently rounded, a woman's cradle for a man's stomach."

Sophie followed Tyler's gaze and found her palm pressed low on her jeans. She lifted her hand, studied her letters and, heart beating furiously, spelled the word *refuse*.

Tyler responded by spelling the word *why*. She didn't even think to object when he used an overturned *M* for the *W*.

"I've had a lot of good times in this cabin. But I don't think anything can compare to what's happening tonight."

Hyperventilation was but a breath away. She quickly searched her letters and spelled the word *won't*.

Tyler's smile faded momentarily, but then he took

two letters, laid them on the board and spelled the word *yes* right on top of another word.

Sophie strained to draw breath to speak. "You can't put a word there."

"I can put anything anywhere I want to." And then he crawled across the board and took her down to the floor on top of her pencil and the crumpled gold bill.

His body blocked the glow of light, making him a silhouette, a shadow, a suggestion of the wolf. Tension tightened the muscles of his shoulders where she held him with both hands. And the proof of their foreplay lay rigid on her thigh.

Ragged breaths brought his chest to her breasts and she tightened willingly. Willing, in fact, seemed to be the word of the day. She was at a loss on how to fight the feeling.

He leaned to one side and the firelight touched his face. His wicked grin made promises that the fingers at her waistband prepared to deliver. He released the button of her jeans, tugged her shirt up her rib cage, then settled his palm possessively on her soft, girl belly.

"This is crazy, you know," he said.

"I know," she whispered. "I don't know you." A tiny moan rose from her throat. "I'm not even sure I know myself. This can't be real."

"It's real," he said as his fingertips slipped under the elastic waistband of her white cotton panties. "And I think in your heart you've known me a long time.

"But maybe you're just now getting to know yourself. Maybe this—" he leaned forward, his long hair draped darkly against his neck "—is who you really are."

And then his sweet-time mouth covered hers.

4

THE GAME OF SEDUCTION was out of control. Tyler knew it the minute his lips settled over Sophie's.

He'd thought to keep the contact quick and teasing, to prove her lips belonged at the head of the kissable class, to assure her they were as soft and accepting as any he'd had the pleasure to know.

But he hadn't expected them to be so giving. Or to keep giving. And with all that giving going on, he couldn't think. He didn't want to think. He wanted to feel.

He wanted to feel Sophie. Her skin, soft to the tough pads of his fingers, smooth beneath his end-of-the-day beard. Her hair, the short blond strands tossed wildly out of control. Her muscles, trembling and tense; her body, taut with urgency, expectant, in need.

He wanted her touch in return, wanted her small hands on his skin, wanted her to indulge, to measure him with her fingertips, to taste the sweat of his sex with her tongue.

What he wanted had become what he needed and it was a damning distinction. One he recognized, one he'd have to face. One growing in proportion to his erection and Sophie's lusty cries.

The sounds in her throat were pleas more than whimpers. They began as a quiver in her chest and rippled upward, swirling through his mouth with desire and her tongue.

He could think of nothing but the way she arched her hips beneath him. The way her hands left his shoulders to work free the snaps of his shirt. The way she managed both while rhythmically plying her tongue against his, arousing him boldly, fully, exquisitely.

She finished with his shirt, tugged it down around his shoulders, spread it open. Her hands made their way into his hair, held him for a kiss that melted all reason, that ripened the skin-bursting tightness in his groin.

He rolled them both to the side far enough and long enough to work free the clasp of her bra. Then he was back on top, shoving her clothing to her neck so her skin touched his from belly to breast.

Her belly was taut and firm, her breasts small, but plump and perfect. He pressed their giving weight with his chest until her nipples beaded and begged for his kiss. But Sophie wouldn't give up his mouth.

She delved deeper, searching, as if there were parts he hadn't yet shared. Her lips tasted, her tongue stroked at his. Propped up on both elbows, he cradled her head, tasted and stroked in return.

He'd never kissed to completion but he knew it was about to happen. Her hips arched and the only clear thought that went through his mind was, *This is a hell of a time not to have a condom.*

She spread her legs wider and he settled deeply, firmly, between. The ridge of his erection lay low on her belly so that when she rocked against him, the rhythm started, making him a slave to his body and the woman beneath him.

A woman he didn't know, a woman he'd seen for the first time today. A woman imprinted forever on his mind.

She raised up and he pressed down and she rubbed and he rubbed back. His erection slid over the silk of his boxers and the friction built with the motion, up and back, up and back, up and...aw, hell, he wasn't going to last.

Sophie's fingers slipped into his shorts. She gripped his backside. He growled in her ear. And at the insistent downward pressure of her hands he pumped and rocked and primed his body with her heat.

Sophie bit at his ear and his jawline, clawed at his back, holding him, urging him, driving against him, crying out sex words and begging and pleading until he felt that first rush of dampness and the squeezing and drawing between his legs. He jerked away, found the tail of his shirt and caught his release.

He took but a minute to breathe, a minute to adjust his shorts, a minute to allow his blood to calm. He was done, but Sophie wasn't and the frustrated motions of her body couldn't be ignored. Neither could the tiny cries of "Please, please," she breathed against the base of his neck.

He raised up, shucked off his shirt, leaned down briefly to kiss both her breasts then grabbed the waistband of her jeans. "Lift up."

She did and he tugged the denim and her panties to her knees. He lay between her thighs, wrapped one arm around and beneath her, kneaded her bottom and spread her open and made her come. Her hands urged him on, as did her cries, the lift of her hips, her fingers in his hair, her sweat.

And when she was wild beneath him, shuddering at his touch, weeping his name, her body pulsing around his fingers, he crawled on top and gently kissed her, telling her with tiny words and soft sounds that the night was early, the possibilities endless.

She came back slowly. It wasn't until he felt her tiny fists balled against his chest, and noticed her whimpers had dissolved into sobs, and her tears wetting both of their faces, that he realized the extent of his error in time and place.

He wasn't usually such a quick trigger, and he should have remembered that sex between strangers wasn't his style. But Sophie had managed to mess with his mind and convince his body this wasn't their first time.

He stood, gripped her unyielding wrists and pulled her to her feet. He tugged her shirt down and her pants up, but he didn't force her to talk or to look him in the eye.

What he did was spin her around and walk her into the bedroom. A red flannel thing lay folded on the pillow. He handed it to her, directed her to the bathroom and closed the door.

Then he returned to the living room and, with frustration a tight knot between his stomach and chest, shoved the love seat halfway to the kitchen and kicked the Scrabble board across the room. Letters scattered across the floor, ricocheted off the footlocker and into the flames.

Hands at his hips, he watched the fire consume the

game of seduction as thoroughly as Sophie had consumed him. But what had consumed Sophie?

The sound of running water reached him above the sound of running rain. Knowing the size of the cabin's water heater, he also knew Sophie wouldn't be able to hide in the shower forever. He didn't intend for her to hide at all. Not until he assured her they hadn't made a mistake.

She'd said this was crazy. It was. But it wasn't a mistake.

Dammit, why couldn't things be as simple as they used to be? For some reason, when he'd come home four months ago he'd expected to return to life as usual, to pick up where he'd left off—seeing old friends, easing into a familiar routine. But Brodie, Texas, wasn't the same.

Except that it was. *He* was the one who'd changed. What he'd wanted at eighteen wasn't what he wanted at twenty-eight.

He gathered up what Scrabble letters remained on the floor and tossed them into the fire. The game was over.

Slinging the flowered blanket around his shoulders, he grabbed his shirt off the floor and headed outside. Huddled deep into the dry warmth, he rinsed the shirttail in the overflow of rain pouring from the eaves.

The thing he hated about mistakes was the way they caught a man with his guard down. Plans would be progressing as smooth as saddle leather when along came a mistake and *boom* those plans were dust, history, and the structure a man had counted on for most of his life lay buried in the rubble.

Of course, his dream wasn't all rubble. Much of it remained fixed on a stable foundation. His career was set to take off, the veterinary practice he'd coveted was only weeks away.

Coming back to live on Camelot was great, even if it wasn't quite the same. He'd been enjoying the heck out of the biscuits his Uncle Jud managed to sneak by Harley. He'd been enjoying the heck out of his three nephews, too.

But his childhood home now belonged to Gardner, Harley and the boys. And rightly so. Gardner's love for Camelot and the land reflected Tyler's own love for veterinary medicine. Besides, he didn't have a lot of use for Camelot now that big brother was building him a house as a coming home present.

The house would've been plenty; he didn't know what he was going to do with the five hundred acres his brother had decided to build it on. Gardner tended to go overboard with his generosity. And Tyler didn't have a doubt that giving spirit had a lot to do with the peace his brother had found with Harley.

Which brought Tyler back to the rubble thing. He hustled back inside and hung his shirt over a kitchen chair. Draping his almost-dry jeans over another, he dried off the best he could with the damp blanket then lowered the heat in the oven and headed for the fireplace.

There was nothing wrong with Brodie, Texas's women. Nothing at all. Not a thing. He liked them as much now as he'd liked their high school versions years ago. And that was the problem. He liked them.

If sparks were to have started with Lindy Coltrain or

Rachel Ford or any of the others who'd been feeding him chicken-fried steak smothered in cream gravy, they would have flared to life long ago.

He wasn't settling for anything but the best in his professional life; why had he thought he'd be able to settle for anything less in his personal?

The change in plans had been destined to happen. Maturity had brought it all into focus. And Sophie happened to be in his line of vision when he'd opened his eyes.

He'd witnessed her mad dash down the cabin road, then seen her slow to a walk once she realized her visitor wasn't a vagrant, that he was the one who had tripped her shotgun alarm.

She hadn't hesitated but headed toward him with *what for* written all over her, her stride steady and uncommonly long for legs that didn't know the meaning of the word.

She was the size of a pixie, a sprite, with raggedly cut blond hair and omniscient green eyes. He'd watched her approach him, assess him, conclude whatever she'd concluded about him.

Then she'd come closer and he'd enjoyed her progress, the way her denim fit, the way she protected her guard dog, the way her small, strong body fought the rough winds.

Later, once he'd learned who she was and what she did for a living, once she'd shed her denim jacket and come closer, giving him a better view, he could see that her muscles came from hard work. Her body was buff, not bulky; sexy, not sculpted. And undeniably female.

What made her seem larger was her temperament. It

hadn't taken him long to realize her energy accounted for most of her size.

And until she'd lain underneath him, until he'd measured the span of her ribs with his hand, until he'd tucked her hips in the circle of his arms, he hadn't realized how small she was, how petite, how vulnerable a woman could be to a man.

How much he wanted her.

He had no intention of letting her escape before exploring the potential of the next several days. He could only think of one way to keep her with him for the night and, now that the water in the shower had quit running, he needed to get busy.

Returning to the bedroom, he jerked the mattress from the frame and hauled it into the living room, placing it between the love seat and the hearth.

He made one more trip, grabbed up the pillows he'd knocked to the floor and wrapped his other arm around the blankets stacked on the bureau. Back in the living room, he tossed the load to the mattress and pushed the love seat in place to serve as a headboard of sorts.

There. She had a choice. The mattress or the love seat. And, unless she planned to sleep on the rope bedframe, they'd be in the same room. Even if he couldn't get her to talk, she'd have to listen. He'd work out what he was going to say once he saw what mood she was in.

"What the hell did you do with my bed?"

Ah. Prickly. He should've guessed.

He turned to find her standing in the bedroom doorway clutching a gray cloth bundle. The red flannel thing hung to her knees and thick red socks slouched around her calves.

She'd scrubbed her face clean of the bare color she'd been wearing and the glitter in her eyes was almost as sharp as the wet spikes of her hair.

"What is my mattress doing in here?"

"My mattress, remember?" He snatched the scrap of gold paper from the floor and pointed out the numbers. "I won."

"You cheated. You can't use an *M* for a *W*."

"Then you cheated, too. Guess that makes us even." He watched her for a long moment, waiting for a change of position, of expression, of the chilly temperature in the room. Finally he wadded the five hundred dollar bill and tossed it into the fire and sighed. This was going to be a long night.

At last Sophie took a reluctant step forward, her lips smashed tight together, and by the time he realized that what she'd been holding was a change of clothes, she'd thrown them at him.

"Maybe you can wear those."

He shook out the sweats and a faded navy cotton T-shirt.

"They're Rico's," she explained. "We worked late one night. I slept in town." When he looked at them instead of answering, she added, "Don't worry. They're clean. I just keep forgetting to return them."

Clean was good, but he wouldn't have minded at all for them to smell of Sophie. "Thanks."

He tossed the T-shirt onto the love seat and pulled the sweats on over his boxers. The fleecy legs were warm and would be a lot more comfortable to sleep in than damp jeans, though snuggling up to female and flannel was preferable.

But since Sophie was still standing there with her arms crossed and her lips disapprovingly tight, Tyler tugged on the T-shirt and held both arms out to the side.

"Better?"

She barely nodded as if the only thing better would be for him to be gone. But he wasn't going anywhere. Not yet. Not until he'd figured out how Scrabble had turned into sex. And why he wasn't as pleased as he had been two hours ago with the knowledge that her crew would finish his hospital by Christmas.

If they hadn't come to terms by morning, well, at least he'd have light to walk out of here by. "You want me to heat up the coffee?"

She shook her head. "It's too late for caffeine."

That sounded like she didn't plan to stay awake and talk.

"I think I'll warm a cup of milk," she said, passing him on her way to the refrigerator.

That really sounded like she didn't plan to stay up and talk. He followed her into the kitchen and watched her pour milk into a white enamel pot. "Looks good. I'll have one, too."

She cast him a sideways glance but went ahead and chugged more milk into the pot she'd set on the burner.

Standing behind her, studying the way the ends of her hair lay close against her nape, the way the shapeless red flannel thing lay soft against her curves, the way the tops of her socks bunched low around her slender calves, Tyler leaned back against the sink and tried to decide where to begin the conversation Sophie obviously didn't want to have.

"Sophie?"

Head bowed, she swirled a wooden spoon through the milk. "This isn't a good time, Tyler. I don't feel much like talking."

Her tight-lipped reaction didn't surprise him, but did have him drawing a contemplative breath. The direct approach wasn't working, so... He glanced to his left and caught sight of Cowboy who'd retreated under the kitchen table.

"We don't have to talk," he lied. "I just thought you might want me to feed Cowboy."

She looked around, her eyes wide as if stunned to realize she'd forgotten to feed her dog. Ruffling her short hair, she said, "I'll feed him," and set to shuffling through the cans on the bottom of the metal pantry shelving.

Tyler watched her mix a can of dog food with a cup of dry. Her movements were economical, but the kitchen was economy-size. He couldn't help but smell her in the air, and that had him shifting positions again.

He braced his elbows behind him on the sink, attempting a comfortable level of conversation. "The way the ol' boy's stomach was rumbling I'm surprised he wasn't over here opening that can with his teeth."

Sophie set the dish near the back door. Cowboy yawned, straightened both front legs and arched his back in a long, drawn-out stretch. Then he slowly made his way across the kitchen floor, his nails clicking on the wooden boards.

Frowning, Tyler followed the dog's casual progress. "Guess he wasn't as hungry as I thought."

"He's hungry. But he's well mannered enough not to

make an issue of it. Besides, he doesn't like an audience," Sophie said, reaching past Tyler into the cupboard for two coffee mugs.

"Either that or the nonchalance is a show of independence."

"How so?"

"If he put on a big production of waiting to be fed, he'd be admitting he couldn't survive without you to feed him. This way he's letting you know he appreciates the offer without losing any of his doggie dignity," he said, moving to stand at the side of the stove and leaning his shoulder into the wall behind.

A smile loosened Sophie's lips. Fighting the grin, she looked down and set both mugs on the stovetop. "Are you a veterinarian or a canine shrink?"

"Actually, I just made that up. Not bad, huh?" He wiggled both brows. She rolled her eyes at his comment, so he went on. "Cowboy reminds me a lot of a dog I had when I was a kid. Her name was Guinevere."

"This was when you lived on Camelot?"

He nodded. "Guin would cock her head to one side, stare at me with those big browns and do everything but tap her foot to let me know she had better things to do than sit and listen to me gripe about my chores."

"I thought chores were a normal part of ranch life," she said, checking the heat of the milk with a fingertip.

"Yeah, but I didn't want anything to do with the ranch." He watched Sophie lick the milk from her finger and tried to remember what he'd started to say. "I was ten when my folks died. Gardner was twenty-two. He was too busy trying to save Camelot to spend a lot of time coddling a pesky kid brother. The dog may have been a gift from his guilty conscience but she was the best thing that ever happened to me."

"Is she the reason you decided to become a vet?"

Tyler glanced over Sophie's shoulder at Cowboy to avoid the probing question, but more so to avoid Sophie's probing gaze. "She was a big part of it, yeah. She got me through a really hard time."

"I'm sorry you had to go through that."

He looked back at her. "Nothing to be sorry for. It happened a long time ago and I got over it not long after."

"You still think about Guinevere?"

"I haven't for a long time."

"Even with all the animals you see?"

"Most of them are working animals, as much ranch hands as the men who run the spreads."

"No family pets?"

"Not in the sense that I needed Guin." Time to get down to business. "Or the way that you need Cowboy."

"I don't need him. He's just..." Her voice trailed; her gaze drifted down to her dog. Her expression settled into one of sweet contentment.

"Tell me about him."

Her head came up and Tyler watched her struggle to find the words before she gave an exasperated shake of her head and poured the milk into the mugs. But he wasn't about to drop the subject now that her lips were moving.

Circling around behind her, he hunkered down and appraised Cowboy with a look he hoped Sophie would consider a professional assessment. "I'll say one thing. He's too well tended to have been picked up as a stray."

"Actually he was."

"Well, you couldn't prove it by me," he said, glad they were finally getting somewhere.

"Thank you," she said, and carried their mugs to the table.

She settled cross-legged into her chair. He took the one directly opposite and sipped the milk he didn't really want, watching while she ran one finger around the rim of her mug, dipping into the froth of bubbles at the edge.

The conversation seemed to have fizzled. But instead of tossing out another prompt, he waited, sitting across from her, sipping his milk. His black jeans hung over the chair to his right, his shirt over the one to his left.

Sophie finally stirred, drawing her knees to her chest and the flannel down to her toes. She cradled her mug between her palms, balanced it on her knees and lifted a stark gaze.

"I was cleaning my mother's apartment, going through her things after she died. I found the litter of retrievers in a Dumpster." She glanced over to where Cowboy lay on the braided rag rug in the center of the kitchen. "He was the only one alive, and so small I didn't think he'd make it. Especially since I didn't have a clue about the care he'd need. Or how to give it."

She brought the mug to her lips, blew across the trembling surface, then gently sipped. Staring into the liquid, she continued. "I thought a lot about his mother. What she went through once she found out her pups were gone. And if whoever left the litter in the Dumpster finally got tired of her, too."

"I'm sorry. About your mother."

Sophie shook her head. "It had been a long time coming."

"It's still never easy."

"Nothing about my mother was easy." Her sharp laugh reflected the bitterness in her tone. "She'd been sick for a while, and worsened progressively over those last couple of years. I went by as often as I could, but I was living away on campus and...well, she wasn't about to move from her home or accept outside help. As long as she was capable of seeing to her own needs, there wasn't much I could do."

"And you're still beating yourself up over it, aren't you?"

She shrugged. "I was going to school full-time, but I still managed to get in a few hours of temp work now and then. As long as I didn't mention the groceries I'd bought, she didn't mention the extra food in her pantry."

"Sounds like you did all you could."

"Maybe. Maybe not. Maybe what I did was all I wanted to do," she admitted, then downed the rest of her milk. Wiping the milk from her lips, she returned her feet to the floor and the mug to the table.

Elbows propped on either side of the mug, she leaned her forehead against the heels of her palms. "At the end, a hospice volunteer came every day. But up until that point my mother refused help. She was never a happy woman."

"Even when you were a child?" Tyler asked, intrigued as much by her willingness to talk as by her tale.

"Especially when I was a child." She looked at him from beneath the tent of her arms. "Life was easier for both of us when I was finally old enough to take care of myself. My father left when I was five and I never could figure why she didn't send me with him."

Tyler leaned back, stretched his legs out under the table, crossed his arms over his chest. "Do you see him often?"

"I haven't seen him since. I used to wait for him to swoop in like a caped crusader and rescue me. When I finally realized he wasn't going to, I wanted to know why, to know what kept him away. After my mother died, I found letters he'd written. Six of them. One on my birthday each year until I turned eleven. He'd asked her to let him make a home for me."

Her sigh was heavy with resignation and a touch of sadness. "I don't know why she didn't let me go. Or if he stopped writing because she never answered."

"Have you tried to find him?"

Nodding, she straightened, braced a forearm on the table and twirled her empty mug with her other hand. "I knew he'd worked construction and I had vague memories of where. I did what I could with that information, but it never seemed to be enough. And entry-level engineering jobs won't pay for a private detective."

"You're an engineer?"

She nodded, added a tiny laugh. "Electrical. With absolutely no practical experience."

"Bet you make a damn good electrician."

"Not that the degree has much to do with the hands-on, but I do. So did my father. From the inquiries I made, I found out he'd been doing the same type of traveling construction work that I'm doing now.

"It may seem like I'm wasting a good education but I love the travel and the uncomplicated life-style. The pay is great and I've socked away enough money that once I find my father I'll be able to go back for my master's."

Tyler latched on to that telling bit of information. "Why haven't you used some of that money to hire an investigator to find your father?"

"Because I can't afford to do both."

"So the degree is more important."

"I didn't say that."

"Okay, then, how long do you plan to put off your degree and continue the search on your own?" She flattened her lips in answer, so Tyler went ahead and intentionally put his big foot in his big mouth. "Sounds a lot like you're avoiding the future, not planning for it."

"Finding my father is very important to me."

"Why?"

"What do you mean, why?"

"You said yourself you haven't seen him since you were five. Haven't had any contact in fact. He did the leaving, he hasn't tried to contact you in fifteen years—"

"That I know of," she interrupted, needing to give her father the benefit of the doubt.

"Okay. That you know of. Your mother obviously wanted him out of your life. But you're not a child any longer. You're an adult with a driver's license, a social security number, a voter's registration. He shouldn't have had any trouble finding you. So, why are you the one looking?"

"Because he's family." She ran an agitated hand

through her hair. "Look, I don't expect you to understand."

"Oh, I understand. It's been just my brother and uncle and me since I was ten. Now there's Harley and the boys, but to tell you the truth, even before my folks died, Gardner and Jud were the only real family I had.

"But life goes on, you know," Tyler continued. "I did. I didn't wait to clear up the past before moving forward."

"And you think that's what I'm doing?"

He rolled one shoulder as noncommittally as possible. This was her confession; for whatever reason, his role was that of confessor.

Sophie came up out of her chair. "Well, I think you need to stick to analyzing animals because you don't have a clue about people."

"Think so?"

"Yes, I think so. The only reason I told you this was so that you'd understand that I'll be leaving soon and why what happened earlier won't happen again. Why nothing will come of it." She settled her hands at her hips. "Why it didn't mean anything."

Silence settled around them, the sound louder than the rain furiously pounding the cabin roof. Tyler dragged air into his lungs; the same air that, minutes ago, had been comfortable to breathe was now resonant with the weight of the stories they'd shared. The source of the tense hum wasn't hard to figure.

Scraping back his chair, Tyler got to his feet, grabbed Sophie's mug and his nearly full one and carried both to the sink. He rinsed the mugs as well as the pan, taking his time, using the sound of Sophie's breathing to measure the urgency in the room.

Finally he turned off the water, grabbed up a towel and walked toward her while drying his hands. "You can say whatever you want, and say it often enough to convince yourself it's the truth, but you'll still be wrong. The real truth is that tonight meant everything and we both know it."

He tossed the towel onto the table. "Now, I'm tired. It's been a long and lousy day. Let's go to bed."

5

GOING TO BED with Sophie didn't turn out exactly how Tyler had hoped.

If Cowboy hadn't been so well-trained, the dog would have been on the mattress where Sophie obviously wanted him instead of camped out on the floor—and there wouldn't have been room for Tyler at all.

He had trouble getting comfortable as it was, what with Sophie curled in a ball at the uppermost edge of the single bed, and the intimacy they'd shared on this very floor stabbing at him like porcupine quills.

If Scrabble hadn't turned into sex earlier tonight, he might not have backed away from her spiny rejection. Instead, he might have enjoyed talking his way out of his T-shirt and sweats and into her warm red flannel.

But they *had* made love, and when Sophie said he was better at analyzing animals than people, she'd been wrong.

He knew she'd been hurt. He knew he'd played a part.

And he'd bet money her distress came from the same place as his confusion. Figuring out how to deal with both was going to take some time.

So, instead of wrapping his arms around her and pulling her close, he spent the night thinking of ways to pierce her prickly exterior, to reach the softness he'd glimpsed when she'd talked of rescuing Cowboy, to find the same openness he'd seen when she'd told of a little girl's dream to be rescued by her father.

Arms crossed beneath his head, he lay on his back and sorted through the evening's discussions, searching the dovetailed ceiling beams for clues while listening to the dog's soft wuffles, the soothing spit and spark of fire, the relentless rush of rain on the roof.

Listening until he heard the sudden catch of Sophie's indrawn breath.

He turned his head to the side, saw her pull her blanket tighter, witnessed the way she reached for her dog, the way she tucked her knees close to her chest and did her best to disappear.

Aw, hell, he thought as tears tracked down her cheeks. He counted them—one, two—as they clung to the curve of her nose—three—and fell—four. Those four tiny tears delivered a sucker punch where buckets of boo-hooing had failed in the past.

This was real and she was hurt. He wanted to hold her and comfort her and tell her he'd been as caught off guard as she. But it was too late.

Time had run out. He needed to go. He couldn't wait, holding out false hope that she'd open up to him—especially when, judging by the small lump of blankets she'd become, he'd soon be sleeping with a dog and pixie dust.

When a rainy gray haze filtered through the window at dawn, Tyler rolled to his knees. He stirred the coals in the grate, made sure Sophie was covered, then grabbed up an extra blanket and draped it over his body.

After fishing his key ring out of the boot where he'd dropped it, he eased the front door open. Cowboy lifted his head. The look in the dog's eyes said, "Thanks, but I'll wait for Sophie." And Tyler answered, "Suit yourself."

The blowing rain soaked the blanket the minute he stepped off the porch. Icy water ran beneath the T-shirt's ribbed neckband and sluiced down his torso, seeping into his drawstring waist. Thick mud oozed between his toes. The legs of the borrowed sweats grew waterlogged as he sloshed through ankle-deep puddles to reach his truck that had sunk to its rims in red clay.

Once inside, he switched on the ignition and tuned in the radio to Camelot's frequency. Shivering, he waited for Gardner to answer. And while he waited he thought of the kitchen at home and smiled at the mental picture of the morning chaos.

He could see the eight ranch hands, who got a big kick out of rough-housing with Harley's boys. The boys, who had the population of Camelot wrapped around their collective little fingers. Harley, who managed the commotion like a trail boss and still allowed Jud to think he was in charge. Gardner, who watched from the sidelines with the goofiest damn grin spread all over his face.

Yeah. That's what family was about. It wasn't about a man who disappeared for twenty-one years without a word to his daughter. Or about a woman who stepped out of the picture and let her daughter raise herself.

Tyler had the strangest feeling that Sophie's search was for what he had at Camelot even more than for her father. And, though she hadn't asked him and he wasn't even sure why the thought crossed his mind, he knew that kind of family was one thing he could give her.

SOPHIE LISTENED to the loud rush of wind and rain as Tyler pulled open the front door. She listened to the crackle and pop of burning wood fed by the whoosh of air up the chimney. She listened to the catch of the latch as the door closed, then the muffled thud of footsteps across the porch.

She didn't wonder where he was going; she didn't have time.

She patted Cowboy's raised head and got to her feet. The dog yawned, stretched and lumbered after her. "I'll take you out in a minute, bud. Let me get some clothes on first."

Leaving the blankets in a tangle on the mattress, she hurried into the bedroom, whipped off her nightshirt and slipped into a pair of jeans, a plain white bra and T-shirt, white crew socks and tan work boots.

She added a hunter green and navy plaid flannel shirt and buttoned the placket to her breastbone, leaving the tails hanging past her hips but double-cuffing the sleeves.

Shoving fingers through hair she was sure had dried to look like a feather duster, she removed her contacts from her burning eyes and slipped on a huge pair of round silver-rimmed glasses.

Now she was ready. Her plain sexless underwear, her big shirt and baggy jeans, her spiky mop of hair and the shield of the wire frames would never inspire interest from a man like Tyler Barnes. The fact that she needed that lack of interest for a safety net was hard to swallow; the intensity with which she needed it an even more bitter pill.

But several times during the past few hours she'd come dangerously close to falling. And she'd do what needed to be done to keep from tumbling into bed with a man she barely knew, a man she certainly didn't love, just to relieve a physical ache of no consequence.

Heading for the back door, she stepped to the side as Cowboy shot past her and off the porch. While he took care of business, she filled his bowl, then washed her hands and gathered up the makings of breakfast for two.

Last night's sex had been the best she'd ever had. If Tyler had made the slightest effort, he could've had her clothes off, had her spread on the warm bed beneath him, had her willing to do anything.

Anything.

That wasn't like her. The two serious relationships she'd had in the past had been short, definitely more cerebral than sexual and, quite frankly, well within her comfort zone.

Tyler Barnes was so far off the scale she didn't know how to rate him. He was dangerously, wildly sensual, a man who knew a woman's body and tempted her recklessly into betraying her beliefs.

Five minutes under Tyler's touch and she'd been willing, desperate, to receive him into her body. They hadn't talked about their sexual pasts; she hadn't cared.

Never again.

Tyler was a temporary distraction, and soon to be part of her past. Her life—her future—was work, the search for her father, her master's degree. These were her objectives. Solid, attainable goals; things she could count on to provide the security and stability she required.

If she hadn't figured in her physical needs...well...at least this way she wouldn't have to worry about neglecting her responsibilities while soothing her lust. Last night Cowboy had been the victim. In the future it might be a weightier obligation. Classes. Her job.

A child.

She stared at the knife gripped in one hand. No. It would never be a child. Never. If nothing else was certain in her life, that one issue was guaranteed.

By the time Tyler's return footsteps jarred the porch, Cowboy had been out and fed and had settled beneath the kitchen table. The oatmeal was cooking and two bowls sat warming on top of the stove.

Sophie concentrated on the knife and the bananas and ignored the pull in her stomach, an expectant tug that tightened with each creak of wet weathered wood.

The latch lifted. The hinges squeaked. Cold wind hissed through the cracks then blasted the door wide open. It bounced once off the interior wall before Sophie caught it on the second inward swing. A spray of water showered her face, misted her glasses, but she didn't have a problem seeing Tyler.

The blanket draped over his head was a sopping mess. He left it in a puddle on the porch and came inside. He stood close enough for Sophie to feel the cold from his skin when he took the door from her hand and, teeth chattering, pushed it closed.

Tiny rivers ran from the ends of his hair and off the shoulders of the T-shirt plastered to his torso. From the knees down, the sweats were reddish brown and heavy. From the knees up...well...the wet jersey fabric was a snug fit. A perfect fit. Even through her rain-speckled glasses she could see how perfect a fit.

At least she could see until Tyler lifted icy fingers and removed her glasses. Then her vision blurred, leaving her other senses alert. When he stepped closer, reached for the tail of her shirt, she felt his cold fingers at her thigh. When he dried her lenses with the fabric, she felt the rasping slide of flannel over the cottons of her T-shirt and bra.

And when he returned the glasses to her face, she smelled the rainy scent of his skin and the impact of his big bad wolf gaze hit her where it mattered. Oh, but his eyes were green.

"Aren't you cold?" she asked, needing a distraction.

"Freezing," he answered, arching a cocky brow.

He leaned forward. She took a step away. He lifted a hand toward her. She backed into the table, picked up a banana and wielded the fruit like a weapon. He laughed, brushed his lips into her hair, then yanked his dry clothing from the back of the kitchen chairs.

Leaving her with a wink and the picture of his jersey-covered backside, he headed for the bathroom, grabbing up his boots and socks on the way, and slapping a trail of wet footprints across the wooden floor.

By the time he returned—showered and dressed as she'd first seen him yesterday, except this time the tails of his wrinkled white shirt hung free—she had the fruit and cereal, the sugar and cream and a pot of coffee set out on the table. She also had all of her emotions completely under control.

"Why don't you leave those in the bathroom?" she said, nodding toward the dirty T-shirt and sweats he'd wrapped in a towel. "I'd planned to hit the Laundromat on my next lunch hour anyway. The extra clothes won't make that much difference."

"I don't think you want this mess—" he lifted the dripping bundle "—in your bathroom."

"I can rinse out the mud—"

He cut her off with a shake of his head. Strands of damp hair framed his neck. "I made the mess. I'll do the laundry. You've done enough already."

"I heated up your soup. Big deal."

"Uh, darlin'. You did considerably more than heat up my soup."

The look in his eyes spoke of intimate knowledge and vivid recollections of "considerably more." Ah...rats. Her body melted, her pulse grew rapid, her breasts pressed points into the cotton of her T-shirt. And here she'd just finished having such a good talk with herself, too.

She looked down, concentrating on scraping oatmeal into both bowls, concentrating harder on holding the spoon and pot handle with sweaty palms, concentrating the hardest on keeping her voice from sounding ready for sex. "Breakfast?"

He laid the armload of clothing on the floor by the door, then pulled aside the curtain to look out the window. "I'm hungry enough to empty a siloful of oats. And it looks like I've got just enough time."

Her hands slowed, her stomach tumbled. "What do you mean, you have enough time? Are you leaving?"

"I radioed Gardner. He's on his way."

"How? I thought he was stranded at Camelot."

"That's the beauty of ranching country. If four-wheel drive can't get you there, four-legged beasts usually can."

She set the pan in the sink, filled it with soapy water, dried her hands on a towel. This wasn't going to be easy. "Tyler, you don't have to leave. I know last night was...uncomfortable but—"

"Uncomfortable? I slept like a rock."

The man really enjoyed being obtuse. "That's not what I meant."

"Oh, *that* uncomfortable." He picked up a banana, split the top, stripped off a length of peel. "Well, Sophie, I hate to tell you you're wrong. But you're wrong." His skilled hands easily skinned off a second strip, a third. "I do have to leave. Otherwise we're gonna finish up today what we started last night. And if you think last night was uncomfortable..."

She could barely breathe for the naked banana. "But the rain. You'll be miserable."

"What's the matter, darlin'? 'Fraid all this sweetness will melt right off of me?" He popped a third of the banana into his mouth.

Not even with a repeat of Noah's flood, Sophie

mused. She arched a brow. "You mean, it hasn't already?"

He pressed a hand to his heart. "Ouch. That's some tongue you've got there. But then—" he grinned "—I already knew that."

She slapped at him with the dish towel. He caught it, of course—cocky cowboy that he was—and tucked it into the neck of his shirt. Then, after burying his cereal beneath slices of fruit, loaded butter and brown sugar on top.

"Mmm-mmm. Nothing like a big bowl of oatmeal and bananas to save a man from starving."

He was so good at sweet-talking she would've believed him if not for the scowl drawing his brows to a vee. She backed into the kitchen area. "Let me see if I can find you something else."

"No, Sophie. This is fine. It won't hurt me to eat healthy for a change." He spooned up a big bite.

"I don't know if I'd call that healthy." His teeth had to be grinding through an inch of sugar. Grimacing, she cast a cursory glance over refrigerator shelves stocked with carrots, cauliflower, cheese, milk and soup. She couldn't even offer him eggs after breaking her last one last night.

She looked back his way in time to see him scoop up another spoonful of cereal covered with caramelized bananas. "I'm afraid it's either that candy you're eating or more soup and raw veggies."

"I'll stick with the candy," he said, and shoveled up bite number three.

He had to be starving and her vegetarian tastes didn't

help. She wasn't prepared to feed a man with this one's appetites. Uh, appetite. She closed the refrigerator, leaned a shoulder against it and sighed. "I'm really sorry."

"For what?"

"Everything. The past eighteen hours couldn't have been any lousier, what with the rain and your truck getting stuck and having to sleep on the floor, and—" she gestured randomly "—being cooped up here with me and my dog."

He pulled the spoon from his mouth, slid it into the bowl, then turned and walked toward her. "Being cooped up here with you and your dog is the most fun I've had in a long time."

"Look—"

"Now, I wasn't talking about the sex, though that was pretty spectacular." His movements were slow and measured, his intent clear.

Sophie's stomach dipped and rolled. The sound of his boots on the floor was the sound of her heart. She told herself to be strong, be strong. "Look, Tyler—"

"I know you don't want to talk about it now, and that's okay. We'll talk about it soon." He came within striking distance, the wolf on the prowl.

Her blood heated and pooled and, with every step he took, anticipation eased toward the edge of fear.

"I've enjoyed getting to know you, Sophie North. You've brought to mind some things I've been meaning to remember. I like that."

She backed into the refrigerator. The electrical hum

sang along nerve endings drawn tight and tuned to his touch. *Be strong. Be strong.* "You do?"

"I do. It's a comfortable feeling," he said, his eyes eager like dark bedroom dreams. He braced his hands on the freezer door then moved in for the kill. He nuzzled her neck, her jaw, the curve of her chin and whispered, "But not as comfortable as I was last night laying my head on your belly."

His kiss tasted of brown sugar, of a sweetness that ran deeper, of yearning. His body came home where it comfortably belonged. She felt the hardness of his thighs and the hardness of his hip bones and the hardness that lay between.

Be strong, Sophie. Strong. When he dipped his knees, settled her thighs over his, she wrapped her legs around his hips and snuggled close. When he parted her lips and his tongue found entry, she shivered.

But when he held her with only his body, wedged a hand between them and covered her breast, she surrendered her strength and came undone.

She pressed herself into his palm, fed on the feel of his fingers, the sweet pull at her nipple, the tingling web spinning from breast to belly.

She wanted more. Needed more. Needed him to fill her emptiness, to soothe the ache that began in her heart.

She needed to be wanted and Tyler wanted her.

A tiny whimper spilled from her lips when he pulled his mouth away. His breathing was ragged, his breath hot and moist against the skin of her neck. "What we're doing may not be crazy, but I'm about to go totally insane."

She settled her forehead against his throat, took in his scent, whispered against his bare skin, "I thought it was supposed to make you go blind."

Slowly, exquisitely, he unwrapped her legs from around his hips and let her body slide the length of his. She felt every muscle, every hard male counterpoint made to fit her female curves.

"I'm glad you find some humor in the situation. But this—" he pulled her hips hard to his "—is not funny."

"No. It's not," she whispered, then knowing she'd regret the admission said, "It's beautiful."

Tyler grimaced like a man in pain. "Don't give me that look, Sophie, or you're gonna be naked on your back on this floor. And I don't think either of us wants my brother walking in on that."

"Your brother?" Just then she heard the bootsteps on the porch. "How did you—"

"I heard the horses."

"I didn't hear anything."

His smile was tender. "Except the sound of my heart pounding in your ears?"

"I thought it was my heart," she said, knowing it was and that it beat with all the strength she had left.

At the brisk rap on the door, Cowboy gave two short yips, roused from under the table, and trotted to the door.

"That'd be Gardner."

Sophie lifted her arms from around Tyler's neck and waited for the guilt, but in its place came acceptance, resignation and a prickle of alarm that oatmeal would never taste as good again.

The knock at the door sounded once more. "I'd better go," Tyler said, and took a step back.

Sophie smoothed down the flannel that had bunched around her waist and used it to polish her smudged glasses. "Yeah. You'd better."

He looked reluctant to leave, more than reluctant in fact. But when he turned away, she crossed her arms over her chest and followed him to the door. The wind brought a blast of rain inside as well as the scent of leather and horses.

Once Tyler stepped onto the porch and out of her way, Sophie got her first look at his brother. They stood about the same height, though Gardner's hat gave him an extra few inches. They had the same green eyes, the same dark hair, but where Tyler's hung long over his collar, Gardner's was cut above his ears. And though Tyler's shoulders were beautifully broad, Gardner's were broader, hinting at the potential in masculine maturity.

Gardner handed Tyler the twin to the long, tobacco-colored oilskin duster he wore. Wrapped inside the duster was a worn but serviceable felt hat. Tyler slipped on the coat then beat the hat into shape and jammed it down on his head.

Gardner looked from his brother to Sophie where she stood in the cabin doorway. A slow, lazy grin spread over his face. "I've obviously been hiring the wrong construction crews."

Sophie took his flirting in stride. "Maybe not the wrong ones, just not the best."

She glanced at Tyler, then, took in the picture of his disreputable hat, his hair caught in the collar of the broad-shouldered coat. His smile was just as lazy, just as slow as his brother's, but his was pure big bad wolf, replete with memories of "considerably more."

"Gardner, Sophie North. Sophie, my brother, Gardner."

She looked back at Gardner then because, though he might be devastatingly handsome, he didn't steal her breath. Tyler did. And she needed to breathe. "My pleasure."

"I have a feeling the pleasure is all Tyler's," Gardner said, and playfully cuffed his brother on the arm. "For a man big on truth you're cutting it close, little brother. You didn't tell me the construction crew member you were stranded with was female. I'd call that a sin of omission."

Fastening the coat, Tyler sent a private wink Sophie's way. "You don't gotta know all my secrets, big brother. I keep the choice ones to myself."

"So I see," Gardner said, turning his speculative gaze her way. "I hope my brother didn't cause you any trouble, Miss North. He can be a real pain—even when he's *not* trying. We've had to quit taking him out in public."

Sophie couldn't help but smile at Gardner's words, or the way Tyler was eating them up. "It was a quiet evening. We had supper, talked, played...Scrabble."

"Scrabble, huh? He didn't con you into playing poker with that deck of marked cards, did he?"

"He tried."

"Yeah, but at least I told you they were marked." Tyler frowned at his brother. "How'd you know about those cards anyway?"

Gardner snorted. "Typical of your generation to think you're the only ones to use this cabin."

"Why, Gardner Barnes. I may just have to tell Harley."

This time his lazy grin spread like wildfire. "Too late. She's already suggested we name this baby Oscar."

Tyler whooped. "You sly dog, you. You know she's gonna kill you for telling."

"Yeah, and I can't think of a better way to die." His grin faded as the tempo of the steady rain approached torrential. "C'mon, little brother. We'd better be going. Sophie's standing here shivering and I've got a day's worth of work to do."

"Ah, yes. Through rain and snow and sleet and hail, a rancher's work is never done."

"Your lazy butt wouldn't know a thing about it. You were always too busy with the animals to do any real ranching." He turned to Sophie then. "Is there anything you need? We can bring back supper later."

The switch from slapstick to solemn caught her off guard—and caught her grinning like a fool. She shook her head, fluffed at her hair. "I've got plenty of food."

"And fuel?"

"And fuel."

He still looked hesitant. "You can ride back with us if you want. Harley won't mind putting you up."

"I'm fine."

"Well, if this doesn't let up by tomorrow we'll be back. We won't forget you're here."

"I'll second that," Tyler said. He dug into his pocket for his keys, slipped one from the ring and handed it to her. His gaze was steady and commanded her attention.

"This is for the truck. You need anything, you get on the radio and call me, okay? It's already tuned in to Camelot's frequency. Just pick up the mike and holler."

He pressed the key into her palm; the metal was warm with the heat of his hand. He stepped closer, leaned down. His eyes had darkened as had the sky; the brim of his hat touched her head and deepened the private shadow.

"Okay," she managed to whisper. She barely managed to breathe. She knew she couldn't swallow, not with her heart in her throat. Not with what she saw in his eyes. Not with the tenderness, the caring, the security, oh, God, not with everything she needed staring her in the face.

She slipped her hand and the key into her front pocket. Then before she did anything she'd regret with the other hand, she slipped it in its pocket, as well.

Gardner cleared his throat, breaking the spell. "It's been a pleasure, Sophie. Hope to see you again soon."

She nodded, hating the way her smile shook, hating even more how she couldn't stop it, and how, after his brother turned to go, Tyler reached up to rub a thumb over her lip.

"You want me to stay?"

"I'll be fine." She gestured toward the cabin. "I've got food and shelter. Fuel. Cowboy."

"But do you want me to stay?"

"I want...time."

"You've got twenty-four hours," he said, and backed a step away.

She nodded, knowing twenty-four hours was barely enough time to put last night into perspective, to deal with the magic of the moment, to reexamine her convictions and determine why they'd failed to keep her safe, to find what remained of her strength.

She watched Tyler go, then, his indecision obvious with every step back. Finally he tucked his head to his chest and pounded down the porch steps. Dodging the worst of the mud and puddles, he took his mount's reins from Gardner's hand and swung fluidly into the saddle.

Sophie glanced from Tyler to Gardner where they sat astride their horses, their shoulders broad beneath the heavy fabric of the oilskin coats. They both huddled deep into their turned-up collars, pulled the brims of their hats down low.

She looked again from one to the other, noting in the expression on their faces a silent communication, a nod here and lift of a chin, and then the verbal as Gardner leaned forward to speak and Tyler leaned to the side to listen.

The rain fell like a mantle of silver leaves around them, the pastures rolled in muted brown-gold waves beyond. The scene was worthy of a McMurtry novel, a

Russell painting. She was the only witness to the unfolding beauty and she was grateful.

Finally, in a choreographed rhythm, Tyler and Gardner reined their horses around and lifted a hand in a brief farewell. She watched them go until her vision blurred—from the mist, she told herself—and the cold rain drove her inside.

And though she sought distractions throughout the day—solitaire with the forty-seven cards she managed to find, hand-washing her underthings as well as rinsing the mud from the clothing Tyler had forgotten—the visual image of the men's departure remained vivid in her mind.

What she found to be the strangest of all was the feelings that picture evoked. She could hardly visualize Tyler without remembering the way he'd loved her. Yet what she felt at his leaving wasn't a physical ache, but...homesickness.

A ridiculous sensation. She couldn't be homesick when she'd never had a home. Homesick implied a loss worth longing for. Her only longings had been of the childhood sort, wishing for what she'd never had. As for loss...

Sophie thought of the six letters she carried in the bottom of her duffel. If there was one thing she regretted losing, it was the chance to make a home with the father who'd wanted her.

And the chance to find out why her mother had refused to let her go.

But homesickness and Tyler didn't go hand in hand. He was not an objective, but an interlude. And Brodie,

Texas, was a black dot on a map of black dots, one of many she'd likely travel through before she found her family.

No, homesickness had nothing to do with Tyler. She was here to build his hospital. If they built a memory, fine. It would make Brodie more colorful than most of her stops.

And if they built a bit of a fire, well, at least it would keep the memory warm.

When nighttime came, her memories of the past and her amateur attempt at philosophy had contributed generously to her confusion, resulting in a whopping stress headache. She left the mattress where it had lain all day, slipped back into her nightclothes, curled up under Tyler's blanket and waited for sleep.

She wasn't sure when it came, if it did at all, if the scent of Tyler was only in her dreams or if it had seeped from the blanket into her skin, if she could wash it away, or if she'd wear it as a memory, if she'd need a memory, if one could forget the first stirrings of love.

6

SLEEP HUNG FAST the next morning. Sophie woke slowly, stirred sluggishly, stretched, and yawned. Remembering foolish dreams of first loves brought her awake enough to poke her sock-covered toes out from under her blanket cocoon. Cold pounced and she huddled back beneath the warm cotton, seeking the remaining body heat. She'd slept too long and the fire had died.

Cowboy's desperate whimpering at the door was her second clue to not only how long but how hard she had slept. She pushed up to her knees and buried her face in the crumpled sheets. Taking a deep breath of Tyler's side of the bed, she raised up onto all fours then onto her feet, savoring the scent of his blanket and doing her best to focus her muzzy mind.

When she found herself squinting against the light streaming in through the window, she realized it was much, much later than she'd first thought. She also realized the rain had stopped. Stumbling to the door to let Cowboy outside, she huddled deep inside the blanket, leaned against the frame, filled her lungs with the near painful bite of crisp, clean air.

And that's when she heard the voices. Not just voices but the sound of rending metal and splintering wood and hammers and heavy equipment. The bridge. Sam must be rebuilding the bridge.

Leaving the door cracked for Cowboy's return—though she figured like a typical kid he'd stay to watch the action up close—Sophie hurried through her morning routine. She brewed a double pot of coffee while slipping into much the same wardrobe as yesterday. But today, with only the slightest hesitation, she chose a barely worn T-shirt of pale sea green.

She filled two thermoses and set them in a bushel basket she'd found on the back porch, adding a tin of sugar, another of powdered cream and the camping mugs she remembered seeing stacked in the back of the cupboard. She didn't know who Sam had with him, but figured these provisions made for a good start.

Shoving an apple and two granola bars into one pocket of her denim jacket, a bottle of water in the other, she picked up the basket and headed outside. Cowboy sat a little closer than she figured. When he looked up and saw her, his doggie smile widened. His tail thumped against the bottom step of the porch as if to say, "Look, Ma. We've got company."

Propping the basket against the wall with one hip, she fished her sunglasses from the breast pocket of her jacket. Better. Now she could see. And when she stepped off the porch, the air frosting her breath, stinging her nose until she sneezed, the first person she saw was Tyler.

At least it was the back of Tyler. And it was an incredible sight.

This morning he wore faded jeans, the legs tucked into knee-high black rubber boots. Mud splattered him from toe to hip. From hip to head the mud thinned, giving way to splotches of water and sweat.

He wore a long-sleeved denim shirt, the cuffs rolled back to show off strong forearms, the tails tucked in at his oh-so-fine waist with a worn leather belt. His hair was held back from his face by a Lone Star Feed and Fertilizer bill cap snugged down in reverse.

She couldn't have said what the others were wearing. She didn't know who the others were, and quite frankly, didn't care. She forced herself to scan the area and wipe the drool from her chin.

Sam and his teenage son Lucas both wore waders. Standing thigh-deep in the subsiding creek, they worked to tear the remaining wreckage of the bridge from its moorings. On the opposite side of the bank, Gardner and an older man Sophie knew had to be the Barnes's patriarch, Uncle Jud, assembled the new framework, laying beams between the tailgates of two trucks.

Sam was the first to catch sight of her. "Good morning, young lady."

"Good morning, Sam," Sophie answered, catching Tyler's near spinning whiplash in her peripheral vision as she set the basket on the open tailgate of his truck.

"Sorry for the inconvenience," Sam went on. "I don't know why this ol' creek had to show its tail in front of company."

Sophie tucked her hands into her jeans' pockets, leaned against the fender and continued to talk straight to Sam. "Don't worry about it. My contract allows for time off in the event of a natural disaster."

Sam jerked the flattened felt hat from his head. "Well,

I'm thinking this disaster has manmade written all over it. I've been knowing those damn bolts were about to give. If I'd've made the repairs when I should've, you wouldn't't've had to miss a day of work. And young Barnes there—" he gestured toward Tyler, then smashed the hat back in place "—wouldn't be needing a backhoe to dig out his truck."

"Hey, Tyler." Lucas pitched a splintered beam to the bank and nodded toward the truck. "A hundred bucks and I'll spit shine that sweet machine for you."

Sophie slowly turned her gaze Tyler's way as he hoisted the beam to his shoulder. He headed up the bank, hitching the load higher as he walked. The tendons in his neck strained against the weight, but his stride was bold and cocky, his bad wolf grin extra bad.

He was glad to see her. And her soft, girl belly was glad he was glad.

"No thanks, Lucas." Tyler tossed the beam into the bed of his truck with the rest of the rubble then stepped closer to Sophie. "No telling where your spit has been. Besides, it's only the bottom half that's dirty. I figure that makes the job worth no more than fifty."

"Yeah, but the bottom half is dirty enough for two whole trucks." Frowning, Lucas moved toward the deep center of the creek, his concern obviously not for his balance as much as for the loss of the extra dough. "And the mud on the undercarriage is gonna hafta be sandblasted off."

Tyler stopped in Sophie's line of vision, blocking her from the others' view. He shamelessly lifted her sunglasses, then tucked them into the pocket of his shirt and took a minute to study her face, a minute to smile with pleasure. A minute charged with anticipation when he ran his thumb over the seam of her lips.

A minute that sapped her strength, rendering her weak enough to respond to his touch with the tip of her tongue.

Groaning audibly, Tyler lowered his hand. His eyes were hot when, staring into Sophie's, he spoke to Lucas.

"All right. A hundred. But no spit," he said, then added for Sophie's ears only, "I'm disgustingly easy. Try me. Please."

"Cool." Lucas's exclamation was accompanied by the cracking of another board.

Sophie couldn't say anything at all. Not with the taste of Tyler on her mouth. Not with that sound he'd made still in the air, still rumbling through her, deep and arousing like a heavy bass beat.

Not with the sudden realization that she'd never be safe—or strong—around this man.

Pulling in a long, even breath, she stepped around Tyler and glanced from Lucas standing in the creek to his father who worked at his side. Then she smiled at Gardner, lifted a hand and waved at Jud before feeling controlled enough to face the enemy.

"How did you end up working on this side of the bank?"

"I planned it that way." The wolf grinned.

She pulled her sunglasses from his pocket and settled them back in place on her nose. "Not a subtle bone in your body, is there?"

"Nope. Not a one."

Shaking her head, Sophie resumed her mission and walked down to the creek. "I brought coffee." She gestured back toward the truck, then called across to the Barnes men, "I'll toss you a thermos. How do you take it?"

"Black'll do," Gardner answered after double-checking with his uncle.

Shucking off his work gloves, Sam headed for the bank, the water sloshing around the legs of his rubber waders. Lucas ripped another beam from the toppled bridge frame, tucked it under his arm like a toothpick and trudged effortlessly toward the truck.

Sophie turned to follow, stopping when Tyler stepped into her path.

"Quit staring," he growled, catching her doing just that.

Teenage muscles were amazing. So was Tyler's possessive response. And her own foolishly weak enjoyment of the same.

She glanced over his shoulder at Lucas. "I'm not."

He pulled her sunglasses down her nose with one finger. All innocence, she widened her eyes.

"Yes, you are," he said, and continued on toward the creek's edge to toss a thermos and two mugs to his brother.

She moved her gaze to Tyler's backside and released a long, slow breath.

"Okay. So I am," she said to herself, then slapped her leg twice for Cowboy and turned to walk down the creek bank, leaving the men to the business of building.

The creek hadn't taken long to recede, though Tyler had been right about the gumbo, she thought, sinking her teeth into her breakfast apple as the soles of her boots sucked at the mud.

Though the moisture in the air gave the wind an icy bite, the sun shone from its winter angle with enough heat to warm her denim jacket. She'd worked in inclement weather often enough to know her face would be windburned if she stayed out too long. Already, her nose was threatening to run. But the day was too beautiful to miss.

A long walk would do her good, especially after yesterday's inactivity. Besides, it would keep her from embarrassing herself in front of Sam and Lucas and Gardner and Jud by rabidly panting after Tyler.

It was a shame that one man had as much going for him as Tyler did. It made it really hard on a girl who was trying to do what she knew to be right. It didn't seem fair to wake up in the morning and be faced with that heartbreaker even before she'd had breakfast.

Sophie sighed. It was inevitable that she'd be seeing him a lot. After all, she *was* building his hospital. And admitting his affect on her went way beyond that of any man before gave her an advantage, made it easier to stage a strong defense.

What she didn't want to do was start looking forward to his visits to the job site, start straining for quick glimpses, plotting impromptu trysts in dark corners. Like a junkie of the worst kind.

Like her mother.

Besides, she had to be fair to Tyler. He had "family" written all over him and Sophie didn't have the time. She just wanted to do her job, continue the search for her father, sock away a little more money for her future, then move on to the next job and repeat the process.

And when she finally found her father, well, she'd take it from there.

She finished off her apple, tossed the core into the matted tangle of brush at the edge of the creek, then pulled a granola bar from her pocket.

Tyler pulled it right out of her hand.

"You scare me like that again and I'll toss you farther than I tossed that apple core," she scolded, her heart pounding.

Unwrapping the second granola bar, she cast a quick glance over her shoulder. She'd walked far enough that the other four men were nearly indistinguishable. "What are you doing down here anyway? I thought you had a bridge to build."

"No building for me. I need these hands for surgery," he said, and crunched down on his half of her breakfast.

She remembered his hands, the calluses, the tender touches. He might need them for surgery but he didn't avoid hard work.

Neither did he keep his opinions to himself, spitting out the bite of granola bar he'd taken. "Man cannot live by sawdust alone. I'm a doctor. Pay attention to what I say."

"I don't know, Dr. Barnes. I'd say most of your patients eat exactly what I'm eating." She pulled the water bottle from her pocket and offered it to him.

He pounced on the lid and poured half the contents down his throat before handing it back. "Exactly my point. You're grazing. Just like my sister-in-law used to do."

"Until you corrupted her with chicken-fried steak and cream gravy, no doubt."

Tyler placed himself between Sophie and the creek bank, pacing his stride to her speed. His rubber boots did battle with the mud, leaving her to maneuver easily on drier ground.

"We don't eat a lot of fried anymore. And I can't remember the last time I had gravy. Harley sort of took it upon herself to clean out our arteries."

Sophie pursed her lips against a grin. "Guess that balances out all that home cooking those willing contestants have you suffering through."

"I'm suffering, all right, but it's all Jud's fault." He rubbed his stomach, right above his belt buckle—a belt buckle that lay flat against the most spectacular abs.

Cowboy flushed a bird from its cover of brush, giving Sophie a safe place to focus her gaze. What she needed was a safe place to focus her mind, she thought, straining to pick up a thread of the conversation. "How could your suffering be Jud's fault?"

"Well, Harley was late coming downstairs this morning, so Jud bootlegged a pan of biscuits. When Harley found all of us at the breakfast table with butter dripping down our chins, she counterattacked with a pot of oatmeal."

"And I'll bet she made you eat it without the caramel topping, didn't she?" She looked up at him from beneath her lashes.

He scowled back. "No caramel, but it wasn't too bad buried under the strawberries and peaches she put up this summer."

"Mmm. I see. Well, I'd better not ever hear you complaining about my cooking again," she said, and playfully punched him on the shoulder.

He grabbed her arm, swung her around and captured her in front of him. "You gonna cook for me again?"

"No. But just don't complain about it." She pushed away and told herself she was glad when he didn't put up a fight. His lack of resistance made it easier for her to stay strong. "I'm sure your sister-in-law doesn't allow you to complain."

"She put up with it for a little while," he said, matching his stride to hers once again. "But then she put her foot down. Told us she'd married into this family and that gave her the right to make sure she didn't grow old by herself while we all keeled over from cholesterol." He shrugged. "I just kept my mouth shut."

"I'd think that would make it rather difficult to eat anything."

He glared down, playfully tugged at a shock of her hair. Then he casually settled his arm on her shoulder. "Jud wasn't too happy having his kitchen commandeered, but he finally gave in and let Harley have her way. He even stopped complaining after she started providing him great-nephews to spoil. I think he decided he didn't want to be the one keeling over from cholesterol—not when he was having so much fun with the boys."

"Tell me about them."

He reached down, uprooted a long straw of grass and stuck the end in his mouth. Then he resettled her in the niche of his shoulder. Closer this time.

"The oldest one, Austin, is nine and has Billy the Kid written all over him. He worships the ground his daddy walks on and is about as reckless as Ben, the second, is reserved. Ben goes about everything with a lot of thought, like he's got a headful of microchips that have to process the data before he can make a decision."

The weight of his arm was pleasing, not possessive or insistent, and so she let him stay. "How old is Ben?"

"He's six. The youngest, Cody, is three. If any of them is a momma's boy, it's Cody. But I think that's because he's around the house most of the time. And because he can't be what he really wants to be."

"Which is?"

"A cat."

When she chuckled, he reached up and tugged on her ear. "That would make Cody your favorite, right?"

"Maybe not favorite, but definitely a boy after my own heart."

"Is she hoping for a girl this time?"

"I wouldn't be surprised if she is, though I know she'll be happy either way. I swear I've never seen anybody as happy as Harley. How anybody that big can be that happy is beyond me."

"The big doesn't last forever, Tyler." And too often there's no happy to go along with it, she silently added. She shifted closer to his warmth and out of the wind and the cold.

"I know. But sometimes I think Harley wishes it did. She loves being pregnant. From the little bit Gardner has said, I guess she didn't have a great childhood. It was a lot like yours, except that she and her sister had two parents to ignore them instead of just the one."

He stopped then and Sophie realized they'd walked far enough to reach the sharp bend in the creek where it meandered through the field behind the cabin.

Tyler moved to stand behind her, slipping his arm from her shoulder to her waist and completing the circle with the other. His chin came to rest on top of her head.

It wasn't a particularly intimate embrace but it made her think of other times they'd been this close, other places he'd laid his head.

When she shivered, he held her tighter. "Cold?"

"A little," she answered, and he held her tighter still.

The sun shone brilliantly, warming her where Tyler didn't, and reflecting off the creek's fast-moving water in facets the color of autumn grasses and the green of Tyler's eyes.

He inhaled deeply and settled her into his body. "You remind me a lot of Harley, you know."

"How so?" she asked, surprised how that pleased her when she'd never met his sister-in-law.

"You're both strong-willed. Maybe a little hard-headed. Definitely women to be reckoned with," he teased.

His deep chuckle rumbled comfortingly down her back. "From what you've told me about her, I think I'll take that as a compliment."

"I meant it as one. She's a hell of a woman." Tyler nuzzled her cheek, settled his lips near her ear and sighed. "A hell of a woman and my know-it-all big brother almost blew it."

Uh-oh. Sophie pressed her lips together. "How so?"

"He wanted a wife, wanted children, but he didn't want anything to do with love. Harley wasn't having any of it. And Gardner came real close to losing more than he realized."

"She was pregnant?" Sophie had seen Gardner. Her question was rhetorical.

"Pregnant and ready to raise the child on her own."

Good for her, Sophie thought. Slipping from Tyler's hold, she slapped her leg for Cowboy to come, and headed toward the cabin. "Better a single parent than an unloving parent."

Tyler took a minute to follow. His rubber boots swished through the crisp grass as he lengthened his stride. "Gardner wasn't unloving. He was so full of it he was about to bust open. He just didn't want to admit it."

"Why?" The question hummed in the air, an active trip wire, tense and twanging, and Sophie waited.

He stepped ahead of her, glanced her way, remained silent until she looked up. Then he pulled the trigger. "Because he couldn't afford to be wrong."

The jaws of the trap began to squeeze. *You can say whatever you want...but you'll still be wrong. The real truth is that tonight meant everything and we both know it.* "How would that have made him wrong?"

"He had this idea that if he let himself fall in love he wouldn't have a mind left to call his own. It was already too late, of course. His mind was mush from the first time they talked on the phone."

The trap tightened. Sophie resisted, increasing her speed and the distance between them. "I'm sure he had a good reason for the way he felt."

"I'm sure he did, too. Which is why when he met Harley it scared him to death." He pulled alongside her again and took hold of her hand. "Sort of the way I scared you."

She pulled her fingers free, reached up and thumped his cap off his head. "Better watch it, Dr. Barnes. The brim of that cap doesn't look big enough to hold in that ego of yours."

"Hey, what's a healthy dose of ego between friends?" he said, snagging the cap from the ground.

They'd reached the back steps of the cabin. Sophie climbed and Tyler followed. Followed until he couldn't, leaving her no room to open the door.

She turned, crossed her arms over her chest and waited.

He reached up, slid her sunglasses from her face. "I heard you cry in your sleep, Sophie. I don't think talking about your folks made you sad, though I could be wrong about that. I don't think it was frustration, though there was enough of that going around. I don't think you're lonely. You're too sure of yourself, too confident. What I think is that what happened between us frightened you. Made you wonder what you've been missing." He traced a finger down her jaw. "Why you're missing it. And if you've been wrong about some things."

The son of a bitch. "What have I told you about analyzing people, Dr. Barnes?"

"I know what you told me. But I also know what I know." He backed off the porch, down the steps and tossed her the glasses. "The first thing I know is that I've gotta get back and help with the bridge. The second thing I know is that now that you've met me your life will never be the same."

She stood there and watched him disappear around the side of the cabin. Then she turned and walked inside, doing a damn fine job of refusing to yell and stomp her feet.

After several frantic trips from the love seat to the kitchen table and back, her jaw aching, her head throbbing and her body rebelling at the confines of the cabin, she forced herself to stop, relax, unclench her fists and breathe.

Damn that Tyler Barnes.

It would be a cold day…a snowy day…hell, the abominable snowman would buy ranch land in West Texas when she was wrong.

What had happened between them didn't serve to frighten her or to make her wonder what she'd been missing. Desire had been ruined for her a long time ago and it would take more than the bad wolf grin of a cocky cowboy to break her heart.

Having regained enough of her strength to venture outside and sit on the front porch, she did just that. She spent the day there, watching the men work—all of the men, not just one. The bridge's center support posts had survived the creek's attack; it was the top timbers that had lost the battle to age and water and split loose from the tethering bolts.

Sam and Lucas threw most of the debris onto the bank on Tyler's side. He stacked it into the back of his truck while Gardner and Jud handled the pieces and the measurements for the new bridge on their side. The five men worked with the effortlessness of a team that had done it often, men who knew one another well enough to predict needs and moves.

Not long after noon, Rico and Dan arrived bearing gifts of burgers and home fries and dessert from Ford's

Diner. After a thirty-minute break to refuel, the men were back at it. Rico and Dan stayed to help. Sophie brewed ice tea, kept fresh water supplied and sliced both the coconut cream and lemon meringue pies for a late afternoon snack.

Autumn dusk came early and Gardner and Jud set up floodlights in the back of Sam's truck. By nine o'clock, Sam was able to drive the plow he used as a grader across the new bridge to haul Tyler's truck free of the mud.

After a round of short goodbyes, and a reminder to Sophie that they'd be at the gate at 6:00 a.m., Rico and Dan headed out. Sam loaded the grader onto his trailer, doused the floodlights and shut them down, and he and Lucas followed. Gardner and Jud left soon after, leaving Sophie with nothing but moonlight and Tyler and the strangest weak tingling in her limbs.

Tyler opened his truck door and, using the light from the cab, soaked a red rag with the rest of the water from Sophie's supply. He tossed his cap to the passenger's seat and cleaned his face first, then the back of his neck and his throat, finishing up by scrubbing the mud-splattered section of forearm exposed between work glove and sleeve.

Sophie stood in the shadows and watched, Cowboy at her feet. She pulled her denim jacket tighter against the cold that frosted her breath and Tyler's. His exhaustion was evident in the slow rise and fall of his lashes. And she had the strangest desire to take him home, run a hot bath to ease his sore muscles, then tuck him in and watch him sleep. Watch him wake in the morning.

It was a feeling she didn't know what to do with so she didn't do anything at all.

He downed the rest of the water in less than three gulps and backhanded the moisture from his mouth. Then he shook his head, blinked to clear his eyes, giving her a glimpse of the big bad wolf and the dimple cut like a shadow deep in his cheek.

"You gonna stand there all night or are you gonna come over here and kiss me?"

He didn't have to ask her twice though she wasn't sure the way she cuddled against him, nuzzled the salty skin of his neck, was what he had in mind. It didn't matter. It was what she needed to do.

He smelled like the great outdoors, like the autumn breeze, the tart tang of growth snapped loose by fresh rain and creek water. He smelled like Tyler, the sweettimes cowboy who'd loved her, the heartbreaker who was making it hard to say no.

She opened her jacket and pressed close. He groaned, nuzzled the top of her head with his cheek, splayed one hand on her back beneath her jacket, the other on her bottom and hauled her close.

"I wish I had a home so I could take you home with me."

She had to give it to him. He had the most original come-on lines. "You have a home."

"I have a home but I also have Jud and Gardner and Harley and Austin and Ben and Cody and that's just too many questions to answer."

She made a move to pull away, but he was awfully strong. And his hand was rubbing wonderfully heavy circles on her back. "I should be insulted."

"But you're not because you know what I meant."

"I'm not because it's a moot point. Even if you had your own home, I wouldn't be going there with you." There, that wasn't so hard.

"Well, I'll have one soon. You'll have to stop by and see it before you leave town."

This time when she pulled, he let her go. "I doubt I'll have the time."

"Make the time. You gotta see this house. Gardner says its a belated graduation gift. I think he just wants me off of Camelot."

Sophie leaned back against the truck's open door and whistled low. "A house? For a graduation present?"

Hooking a boot heel on the running board, Tyler boosted himself into the driver's seat. "What it really is, is a celebration of the fact that I turned down the big city and came home. I guess I stayed away long enough that Gardner got worried."

"You never thought about setting up your practice anyplace else?"

He gave her a funny look. As if he didn't understand the logic behind her question. "Why would I, with all I had waiting for me here?"

"And what did you have waiting for you?" Sophie asked, thinking about her day of graduation, how she couldn't wait to go. Anywhere. Away.

"Friends. Family. Heck, most of my friends are like family." He massaged a hand over the back of his neck. "You live in a place all your life it's like you got kinfolk from one end of the county to the other."

Sophie glanced down at Cowboy, wondering—but only briefly—if she had kinfolk anywhere. "The longest

I ever lived in one place was the four years I spent in college. And those four years were temporary."

"You and your mother moved a lot?"

"Every six months as regular as clockwork. Not necessarily a new city each time, maybe just a new—" hovel, she wanted to say "—apartment."

"Did she have trouble settling down or just trouble holding a job?"

"She never had a job. What she had was men. They gave her what she needed. Either a roof over her head or the money to provide one." And one of them gave her what eventually killed her, Sophie thought bitterly.

Tyler braced one elbow on the seat back, the other hand behind him, straightened, stretched, arched his back. Once he'd worked out the kinks, popped joints and vertebrae, he rolled his neck in an impressive stall tactic before stating, "Well, that makes sense then."

"What makes sense?" she warily asked.

"Why you're so determined to find your father." He pressed a thumb to her tightly pursed lips. "I know. I'm analyzing again."

"Yeah, so stop it."

He stopped it. For a minute. Then arched a brow and dared her to deny the conclusion he'd drawn.

She blew out a long breath that plumed in the cold and the light from the moon. "I want to find my father because he's my family. Simple as that."

Tyler's smile was tender. "You never had a home, Sophie. You may be looking for your father, but what you're searching for is the stability you were denied as a child."

She'd been wrong. His smile wasn't tender. It was patronizing. Know-it-all. And too perceptive. The reasons she did what she did were nobody's business but her own. "Look, Tyler. I'm searching for my father. You're searching for a wife. You may not like my reasons. I may not like your methods. But you know as well as I do that neither of us will change our mind due to the other's opinion."

Tyler grew still, the moment uncomfortable, the interior light shining cold above his head. Finally he moved, lifting one foot and pressing the toe of his boot to a button on the truck's metal frame to extinguish the cab light.

From the darkest of shadows, he asked, "What's wrong with my methods?"

Sophie laid a hand on Cowboy's head. "You mean, your grand scheme to sample the wares of the local bachelorettes?"

Tyler blew out a disgusted puff of breath. "You make it sound like the dating game."

"Isn't that what it is? Isn't the entire seduction process one big roll of the dice? One deck of marked cards?"

"One *M* used for a *W*? An illegally played word?" He shifted on the seat. "Samplin' wares and home cookin' is all about foreplay, Sophie. It's no different than a game of Scrabble."

"What about friendship first? What about common interests and goals? Why does everything have to be about—"

"Sex?" he filled in for her. "Because that's what men and women do. They make love."

She turned her head sharply, stared into the black

night, listened to the creek water run. "Or they call it that, anyway, to make it look pretty when what they're really doing is trading, negotiating, or satisfying lust."

"Considering what you lived through with your mother, I can understand if sex makes you...uncomfortable. But you didn't seem too hung-up the other night. At least—"

"Yeah. Until I realized what we'd done. People who've known each other three hours can't make love. It's an impossibility." Even though she'd called it that and known that he had loved her well.

She turned back then and wished she hadn't. The moonlight shone directly on his face. His dimple had vanished along with his smile, and the tiny lines that spread from his eyes in a sunburst of humor were now deep, solemn grooves in his skin.

"So what do you call what we did?" he finally growled. "You say it wasn't making love because we haven't known each other long enough for that. And, if we're working for accuracy here, you can't call it sex because we didn't *do it.*"

He was angry. Or hurt. Probably a combination. His voice alone would have convinced her. She didn't need the added proof of that look in his eyes telling her what he was feeling wasn't a bruised ego as much as it was a bruised heart.

Rats. She was going about this all wrong. But he'd started it with his unqualified psychoanalysis. And she'd finished it simply by not leaving well enough alone.

She stood straight and used all her strength to face him. "What we did was...felt...great. But that's all it was. Feeling. Physical feeling. There wasn't any depth. Any...emotion. Or any rational thought."

"Sex doesn't have to be rational. The only time it is rational is when breeding's involved. Other than that I'd say it's pretty damned irrational, in fact."

"And you think it's okay for your body to take over your mind that way?"

"I'd love for my body to take over my mind." He turned forward in his seat, away from her. "Hell, I live for my body to take over my mind. In fact, a long hot night of mindless sex, would do me a lot of good right now. But it's just not happening these days."

His grousing and grumbling brought a surge of tenderness. "No new invitations for chicken-fried steak?"

"As a matter of fact, I have one for tonight." He slammed the door, turned the key, gunned the engine. The dark window buzzed down, showing his face in sharp silhouette. "If I hurry home and shower, I'll only be thirty minutes late. And I won't even have to heat up my gravy."

She watched him spin out in his truck. Felt the rooster tail of mud splatter her shins. She knew she'd made her point. She'd won. She was right and he was wrong.

So why didn't this feel like a victory?

7

THE CLOUDY END of November rolled into December's chilly days. Sophie continued to see Tyler on a regular basis, but only at the job site. He said nothing of their conversation that last night at the cabin, so she said nothing, either. Both tacitly agreed a working relationship was no place to hash out anything personal. And so their private moments remained buried.

They talked of the everyday instead. Of the way Tyler's eyes lit up with pleasure as the construction progressed. Like a kid with a Tinkertoy, Sophie teased him, before demanding to know why anyone would need the number of electrical outlets he had scattered around the surgery and examining rooms.

He razzed her in return, asking if she planned to file a grievance, going on to explain the requirements of the specialized equipment he'd ordered to reduce his patients' time in the hospital, so he could be back in the field where he was needed.

She asked about the progress on his house. He asked about her search for her father. When she told him that Cowboy was due for a rabies booster, he escorted them both to the clinic and on the way told her of Harley and Gardner's new daughter, Dani.

Except when he stopped by after hours, Sophie didn't take a lot of time to visit. After all, he *was* paying her sal-

ary. She owed him a full working day. But even with
minutes stolen here and there, their friendship couldn't
help but blossom.

The roots of their relationship—the forced isolation,
the heated kisses, the game of Scrabble—made for an
intimately strong foundation. Like any formed in the
midst of a disaster, she ruefully thought.

Whether their disaster was truly natural, or manmade as Sam had suggested, she felt stronger for the experience. She'd come face to face with the wolf and held
fast to her convictions, suffering only a minor lapse of
weakness—one tiny wish that her life had been different, so she could be different.

But she was who she was and the moment had
passed.

At least she thought it had passed until Tyler started
dropping by the cabin bearing gifts, leaving them on
the porch for her to find in the evening after work.

The first was a box of empty shotgun shells and a car-
ton of rock salt. The note attached said, "Better safe than
sorry." The second was a basket of ruby red grapefruit
and oranges from the Rio Grande Valley. That note
said, "Cholesterol is a bad thing." The third time he left
a deck of cards. He also left a note that said, "To help
you kill the long lonely nights."

She could've killed *him* for that one.

She had a lot to keep her busy at night. Just because
she spent four evenings marking the cards and learning
to cheat at solitaire didn't mean she had no better way
to spend her time.

By the time the building was finished, she'd reached
the point of fidgeting on Rico's truck seat during the

ride home. Of burning with impatience to see if Tyler had been by. Of being disappointed if he hadn't.

On evenings when her porch was bare and the moon full, she walked Cowboy down the creek bank, listening into the night for that flashy red truck to rattle the timbers of the new bridge.

In fact, she started looking forward to his visits to the job site, started straining for quick glimpses, plotting impromptu trysts in dark corners.

So it was a good thing it was time for her to go.

SOPHIE WAS LEAVING and Tyler was miserable. He hated the feeling. Hated even more admitting it was there. What he should have been feeling was relief that her distracting presence would no longer be interfering in his plans.

But his plans had changed. And he was about to lose the best thing he'd ever known.

He owed her an apology for his behavior that last night at the cabin and had wondered if he should blurt one out, get it out of the way and all that. But he figured his tongue would get tangled and instead of telling her he'd been exhausted and hadn't known what he'd been saying, he'd tell her he'd been frustrated, wanting her in his bed and in his life and then they'd be back to arguing about sex and family and his marriage and her father.

So he decided to show her what he couldn't find the words to say. He started with small gifts. Tiny inside jokes with deeper meaning. He'd offered protection. She'd thanked him for the shotgun shells. He'd told her figuratively how glad he was that she wouldn't be keeling over from cholesterol. She'd told him literally that she was a goner for fresh fruit.

And when he'd tried to explain that an evening spent in his company would be better than one spent alone, she'd asked if he knew how hard it was to cheat at solitaire. He didn't know which one of them was better at playing games.

What he needed to do was sit her down and tell her face to face that the "willing part" of a relationship was nowhere near as important as sharing dreams. That he'd found what he'd been looking for without looking. That he wanted to be her family, wanted her to be his wife.

And he needed to tell her today because his time was running out. This was his last chance to convince her that he was worth the risk.

He pulled his truck to a stop in front of the old clinic and parked. DayLine had completed the initial build-out of the new hospital. Only the finishing work remained. The floor tiles, the painting and the last-minute details would be handled by students in the high school co-op program. The installation of equipment Tyler would take care of himself.

Waving at Doc Harmon's receptionist, Annette, as she pulled her pickup out of the lot, Tyler walked around to the back of the building where the DayLine crew busily secured equipment. Rico and Dan fought spools of electrical cable into the bed of one truck. J.D. wrestled to secure a trailer to the uncooperative hitch of another.

Cowboy snoozed on a worn patch of packed dirt near the hospital's front door. As Tyler approached, the dog opened one eye, closed it, never moving from the sun-warmed spot. Tyler let the sleeping dog lie, knowing Sophie couldn't be far away.

He found her on a ladder in the surgery, her feet spaced one rung apart for balance as she coiled an extension cord from elbow to palm. She was dressed in her usual uniform of white T-shirt and jeans, a uniform whose simple lines flattered her body.

A tool belt hung low on her hips, tugging the waistband of her jeans over the swell of one female hip. Though her hard hat covered all but the longest strands of her hair, he didn't have a bit of trouble distinguishing her from the rest of the crew.

How could she have ever imagined otherwise?

He leaned a shoulder against the door frame and watched her work, enjoyed the way she clamped her lips in concentration, remembered the feel of those lips on his own.

He shifted then and she heard him, slowed her motions and smiled. It was that smile that kicked him in the gut every time. That and the breathy little, "Hey," she drew out in greeting.

She turned her attention to the cord and backed down the ladder, tossing the coil into the bottom of a wheeled toolbox that sat in the far corner of the room, and adding wire strippers and cutting pliers and insulating tape until she didn't have anything left to add—and no reason not to turn and face him.

"We're, uh, getting ready to go," she said, pulling off her hard hat and fluffing up her flattened hair.

"I know." He shouldered off the door frame, jammed his fists into his pockets. "I came to say goodbye."

"I'm glad. I wanted to thank you." When he frowned, she added, "You know. For the presents."

"You've already thanked me."

"Maybe for the gifts, but not for the gesture." She worried her hard hat, shifted it from hand to hand, her knuckles as white as the fiberglass. "I knew what you were doing. And I figured out why..."

"But you didn't say anything because you didn't want to deal with it," he said, and moved into the room. One step, then another. Closer, closer. Close enough to sense her trembling, to see the rapid rise and fall of her chest, the wild pulse in her throat. He pried the hat from her hands, placed it on the toolbox then pulled in a deep breath full of her scent.

"It's just not the right time. I mean—" She shrugged, averted her gaze, then began fumbling with her tool belt. "You're just starting your practice. Your hospital's nearly operational. You have a new house. A new career." Her lip lifted in a wry smile. "Your choice of the daughters of Brodie, Texas. You don't need..."

He moved his hands to her waist and unhooked the tool belt that was giving her so much trouble. He had a little trouble of his own, what with her breath stirring his hair and her hands hovering over his and her body so near.

Inhaling a second deeper time, he slid her tool belt from around her waist and dropped it beside the hard hat. Then he took a safe step in reverse. "I don't need what?"

"You don't need anything standing in your way." Pursing her lips, she pulled herself up to her full height and crossed her arms over her chest.

He had her on the defensive. Defensive was good. It meant this moment of truth wasn't any easier for her than it was for him. Uh, at least he hoped that's what it meant, that he wasn't the only teenager here tripping over his tongue and fast-growing body parts. "Anything? You mean, like you?"

She lifted one shoulder, lifted her chin. "Yeah. Like me."

"What makes you think you'd be in my way?"

The sound she made was one part laugh, one part huff and all parts sarcastic. "Do you want the reasons in alphabetical order? Or just a random list off the top of my head?"

"You have that many?"

"I have that many." She enunciated each word clearly, distinctly, exactly.

He wondered which of them she was trying hardest to convince. "All right, then. Let's hear 'em."

"Okay. How's this for starters? I don't deal well with permanence. Everything I own is either in my duffel bag out there in the truck, or stored in an eight-by-eight warehouse in Houston. My only address is the company address. What little bit of mail I get is held for me there."

If all her reasons were so flimsy, this would be a piece of cake. "This isn't a loan application, Sophie. I'm not asking for a list of your assets, a permanent address or references."

"Well, why aren't you? We're talking about your future here. Six weeks ago we hadn't even met. Now you want to explore this...this—" she gestured wildly

"—this thing we have between us and you don't even know me."

"I know enough to want to know more."

"What's that supposed to mean?"

"It's not that hard, Sophie. So, I don't know your favorite color, your astrological sign, if you love classical music and hate rock 'n' roll. But I do know that you're independent and strong-willed and protective of your guard dog." She smiled at that, so he pressed. "Tell me more. Tell me what I don't know. What you think I should know. Tell me why this thing between us won't work." *Tell me the truth, dammit. The truth.*

"All right." She seemed to need a minute to think and used that minute to sidle up beside the ladder.

As if six feet of wooden slats would keep him from doing what he could to stop her from leaving.

"Okay. Here's another reason."

"Finally." He forced a look of exasperation. "I was growing old here."

She scowled right back. "My job. It requires constant travel. And it's a job I like. One that meets my needs. And I can't give it up because it's provided the best leads yet on my father. I can't make any major changes in my life until I find him. You know how important this is to me."

He moved in, bracing one boot on the ladder's lowest rung, leaning an elbow on another, trapping her between the ladder, the wall and his logic. "You're giving me surface reasons, Sophie. Things that are easy enough to work around."

"They're not that easy, Tyler. Not all of them, anyway. And not any of them without more work than you have time for."

"Why don't you let me decide what I have time for?"

"Tyler, you need a wif...a relationship with a woman who can make you a home." She reached out with both hands, then pulled in on herself and pressed her fists to her chest. Her shoulders drooped as she leaned back against the wall.

"I can't do that." Her voice barely reached to a whisper. "Don't you see? I just...can't."

She was so tiny. And she was hurting. Her eyes glistened, but she didn't have it in her to cry. Wouldn't even think to cry, dammit, because instead of even entertaining the possibility that he might be what she needed, she was thinking of how many ways she could ruin his life.

Her selfless spirit had him itching for a fight. "What about you? What about what you need? Do you ever think about that, Sophie?"

She nodded, but it looked like a no.

"What if you're wrong?"

Her chin came up. "About what?"

"About everything. What if this *is* the right time? The *only* time? What if you'll never have another time?"

She pushed away from the wall, pushed on past the ladder and waited until she stood safely in the center of the room to turn. "I wish I could give you what you need, Tyler. But I can't. I'll live with this moment for the rest of my life. I'll always wonder. Not about being wrong, but whether I was right.

"You've got to understand. Sex is so tied up with the bad stuff in my life that I don't know if I can ever trust the heat we create. You deserve more, Tyler. You deserve a sure thing."

"And you don't deserve anything? You don't deserve love?" He was desperate now. This was his last chance and, dammit, he wasn't going to lose. "C'mon, Sophie. Tell me you want to go. Tell me you don't want to take this heat all the way. Tell me you won't regret leaving here knowing you left this unfinished."

She didn't say anything, but she didn't have to. Her sad eyes said plenty. He turned away with a curse, knowing he'd been handed a battle he couldn't fight in the minutes he had left. He doubted he had time to regain the ground he'd just lost.

"Aw, Sophie," he began, rubbing away the pounding at the base of his neck. "I don't want to fight. I want—"

A heavy crash interrupted. Metal scraped against metal. An eerie unending screech sliced the air. He started forward. Stopped at the sound of shouts and pounding feet. Looked up over Sophie's head.

"I saw him come in here," one man yelled.

Then Rico's voice, "He's in the surgery. With Sophie."

Seconds later, Rico slammed to a halt in the doorway. Tyler was already halfway across the room. He didn't like the look in the foreman's eyes. Didn't like it at all. "What happened?"

"Dr. Barnes. Out front." Rico lowered his voice. "Now."

The Latino's expressive dark eyes avoided Sophie's and his quiet calm set Tyler's pulse racing. That, and the way Rico had called him Dr. Barnes which he hadn't done since that day they'd worked together on Sam's bridge.

Aw, hell, he thought, his mind denying what his gut somehow knew.

"What's wrong, Rico?" Sophie asked, her voice flat, her tread silent as she moved to Tyler's side.

Rico stepped into the room and stopped her forward motion with a gentle grip to her shoulder. "You might want to sit this one out, *güerita.*"

At that, Tyler headed through the door. He glanced back once and saw Sophie try to jerk free, but her foreman shook his head and held fast. Dread seeped into Tyler's blood and he prayed as he'd never prayed before.

Then Rico's voice reached his ears. He heard one word. "Cowboy." And Sophie's wail echoed off the walls.

By then he was running, shouts and curses and the sound of Sophie spurring him on. Once outside, he struggled to take in the chaos. The trailer J.D. had been wrestling to hitch to the truck was now butt up against the hospital. The weight of the Ditch Witch loaded on top had taken the trailer up on two wheels. The equipment itself lay on the ground where Cowboy had been.

Where Cowboy still was. Shit.

The trailer sat at an evil angle, the weight of the toppled equipment canting it dangerously to one side. Wheels that should've been on the ground were spinning in the air. And somewhere underneath all that wrecked equipment was Sophie's dog.

He scrubbed back his hair, rushed around to the exposed underside of the trailer. He pushed, testing the stability. The trailer shook, groaned, the Ditch Witch slid another six inches.

Damn. If it moved any farther, all the veterinary education available wasn't going to do Sophie's dog a bit of good. "Can we see about bracing this thing somehow?"

"Dan. J.D. Get over here. Help me with the trailer," Rico ordered. "We'll use it as a lever. The rest of you get ready to lift that hunk of metal out of the way."

Tyler looked up. The DayLine foreman stood on the concrete walkway, blocking the hospital's front door. Behind him, Sophie still struggled to escape his hold and the building.

"But, Rico," J.D. replied, drawing Tyler's attention. "We lift the Ditch Witch from where it's laying, it's gonna ruin—"

"*Dios mio!* I don't give a damn what gets ruined, J.D. Just get your ass over here. We've got to get the Witch out of the way and we don't have time to be pretty about it."

The men moved into action. Tyler dropped to his knees under the high end of the trailer and swore at the mess beneath.

"If you give me three inches, I think I can pull him free," he called up to Rico, hoping he didn't do the dog more damage by moving him. Not that he could considering the way the equipment looked to have slammed him into the wall before burying him under more weight than a dog was built to bear.

Rico, Dan and J.D. moved in and pulled down on the trailer's side. The leverage lifted the Ditch Witch. One inch. Two. Tyler crawled farther under the trailer. The metal screamed, scraped. The men groaned. His own breathing echoed in his ears. But as hard as he listened, he couldn't hear the dog.

He couldn't hear the dog.

He wrapped his hand around Cowboy's collar, buried his fingers in the ruff of the labrador's neck. The minute he felt clearance, he pulled, praying that what he'd just felt on his wrist was warm breath and not just a blast of hot air.

"Easy, boy, easy," he crooned, sliding the eighty lifeless pounds slowly and only as far as he needed to have clear working room.

He squatted, slipped a hand up inside Cowboy's thigh to check his pulse. Found it weak, thready. Not good. Not good at all. The dog's breathing was shallow and rapid. His gums way too pale.

Tyler took a deep breath, glanced up, found Sophie hovering, her lips white, her eyes wide. *Aw, hell.*

"Sophie. My keys are in the truck. Find the one that opens the clinic. Rico, go with her." *Keep her busy*, his eyes added.

Rico nodded and took Sophie's arm again.

"Tyler, what—"

"He's shocky. I need to get him stabilized. Then we'll take it from there. Now go," he ordered, and Sophie ran.

By the time he hefted the eighty-pound dog across the construction site and into the clinic, Tyler had mentally outlined the next few steps he needed to take—and where to go from each should one effort fail.

"Sophie, hit the lights," he said, and she did, trailing

one step behind as he carried Cowboy to the treatment room and placed him on the stainless steel table.

Damn, he wished the new hospital was operational. Not that Doc Harmon's facilities weren't adequate. They were. Hell, his own dogs had been treated here. But this was Cowboy, and Sophie deserved the best.

He pulled open the first cabinet, found blades and syringes, moved to the second and found the tubing he needed. He started an IV drip and administered steroids, then covered the dog with a thermal blanket that had seen better days.

"Tyler?"

"In a minute." While he adjusted the drip of the IV and double checked the dog's pulse, he cut an entreating gaze to Rico.

"C'mon, *güerita.* Let's let Dr. Barnes do his thing in private."

"I'm not leaving."

"Then I'm not leaving with you. But we're gonna not leave back here out of the doctor's way, okay?" Rico nudged her toward the door.

It was better than nothing. Tyler knew she wasn't going to budge any farther. He rolled the examining table to the booth sectioned off at the back of the room and transferred Cowboy to the X-ray surface.

While waiting for the film to develop, he moved the dog back to the treatment room and drew blood. Then he went to pull the X ray, snapped it into place on the viewing screen and swore.

"Tyler?"

"Not now, Sophie." The rib cage was a mess. The

chest cavity was full of free air. There was no way for the lungs to expand.

"I've got to get a chest drain in." He turned from the viewing screen, looked from Rico to Sophie and back. "I could use some help with the IV and the bandaging."

Rico stepped forward. "Hey, man. Whatever you need."

"No." Sophie walked to Tyler's side. "I'll do it."

Her voice was steady and he had faith her hands would be, too. As long as he didn't have to look at the silent tears running down her cheeks, they could do this.

He rummaged through the cabinets and found the instrument packs and the gauze and bandages he would need. Then while Rico stood by and watched, Tyler moved Cowboy into the surgery suite and showed Sophie what to do.

TYLER CUT OFF the fluorescent overheads, leaving the under-the-counter lights burning low. Cowboy was resting quietly. He'd be due for another blood count soon, but until then Tyler intended to catch a short nap.

He had to force Sophie to the door of the treatment room. "That's all I can do for tonight."

"I'm not leaving."

That didn't surprise him a bit. "Sophie, you're tired. Let Rico drive you back to the cabin. I'll get a room at Ford's and come up and check on him every couple of hours."

"Fine. You do that." She crossed her arms over her chest. "But I'm not leaving."

"What good's it going to do you or Cowboy for you

to exhaust yourself?" And she was exhausted. Her hair stood on end. Tiny half moons bracketed her mouth. Even the circles under her eyes were bruised.

She barely managed to shake her head. "He might need me. I have to be here if he needs me."

He wanted to tell her that if Cowboy needed anyone during the night, he would need a doctor. But that wasn't quite true. The emotional bond between animal and owner was often times as powerful as medicine.

"Okay, then. Come with me. I'll get two rooms. You can ride over when I come back."

"I can't go off and leave him lying there, Tyler," she said and silently walked back to the ICU pen where Cowboy rested. Her fingers closed around the wire mesh door. "He's cold. And he's alone. I know he can hear my voice.

"If he doesn't make it," she whispered, "if he...slips away during the night, I have to be here. He has to know that I loved him, and that I tried."

Tyler closed his eyes and tried to numb his mind. He was a doctor, he had to be objective. But Sophie's grief sliced him up, leaving his heart open, a raw, aching wound.

He wrapped his arm around her shoulders and pulled her close, needing her comfort, but needing even more to offer the same. "C'mon. There's a couch in the reception area. We'll go sit out there for a while."

He had to physically turn her around, but finally she went with him. They found Rico on the couch, sitting forward, his elbows braced on his knees, his hands knotted together between.

He looked up sharply when they entered the reception area. "Anything new?"

Tyler shook his head. "It'll be touch and go for a while. The chest drain will need to stay in twenty-four to forty-eight hours. And I've gotta keep a close eye on his red blood count."

Rico's glance took in Sophie's condition. His frown deepened. "But no bad news is good news right?"

Tyler rubbed a hand down his face. Why did this always have to be so hard? "Right."

"I guess I'll head out. Catch a bite to eat. Make sure the crew got loaded up. Check on that damn trailer..." He got to his feet, shoved a hand through his thick hair, blew out a long breath. "You gonna be okay, *güerita?*"

She nodded, wiped at her eyes and Tyler held her tighter.

Rico approached, standing as tall and as protective as Tyler. "I'm gonna wait and pull out tomorrow. I'll talk to you in the morning and we'll decide what to do, okay?"

She stepped from Tyler's arms into Rico's and hugged. "I'm not going without him," she said, her voice muffled against Rico's chest.

"We'll talk tomorrow," Rico said, and returned her to Tyler.

"Thanks for your help." Tyler offered the hand that wasn't holding Sophie and Rico's return grip was firm in its warning.

"I wouldn't do it for just anyone, man."

"I know. I'll take care of her."

Once Rico was gone, Tyler settled back in the corner of the vinyl cushions. He squirmed until the metal armrest wasn't digging into his ribs, then reached for Sophie's waist and pulled her down beside him.

She pulled up her knees and curled into his side, plucking at the three metal buttons on the placket of his navy T-shirt as if the tiny, repetitive motion kept her centered, held her together.

He brushed her hair back from her face, brushed aside his body's reaction to her hands. When he thought of what was happening here, what she was going through, how she was seeking strength from him, his heart took off, and the surge of protectiveness that welled inside stole the rest of his breath.

"You okay?" he managed to ask.

She gave a small laugh. "I don't think I ever want to love anything again."

He wasn't quite sure—

"I mean, I know caring for a dog isn't the same as caring for a person." Her sigh was a deep shudder. "But I can't imagine anything hurting the way this does."

Oh, darlin', you're breaking my heart. He continued to stroke her hair from her face. "Cowboy's your best friend, Sophie. Of course it's going to hurt."

"He is my friend, isn't he?" She settled deeper into his side. "He's the first animal I've owned, you know. When I was younger, I wanted a cat. I figured a cat would be perfect."

"Why perfect?"

"A dog would be too noisy. My mother would hear it and that would be the end of that. I thought off and on about a turtle," she said, sliding the buttons in and out of the holes. "A turtle would've been quiet, but I didn't think it would put up with a lot of cuddling.

"Besides," she continued softly, "if something happened to me, I knew a cat would be independent enough to take care of itself."

Tyler's hand stopped midstroke. "Why did you think something would happen to you?"

"The odds mostly. Sooner or later a kid who roams the streets gets picked up or hit on. I saw it happen. A lot."

"It didn't scare you enough to keep you home?"

"Nothing was going to keep me home." Her hand stilled on his button, then crept up to his neck and held him tight. "But then, no one tried to keep me there."

He waited for her to continue. She'd grown quiet, as if she was thinking, and he waited. But she didn't say more and her breathing steadied and grew deep.

Emotional exhaustion was a wringer. He hoped her sleep would be sound. She'd need the rest tomorrow when the real waiting began.

Or when the grieving began.

At this point he wasn't placing bets.

8

DAMN.

Cowboy's red blood count was not looking good. Not good at all. Tyler had just run out of "wait and see" time. He was going to have to go in before the dog grew weaker and hope didn't matter anymore.

It had been the wee hours when Sophie had fallen asleep. Miraculously, she hadn't stirred since. Considering her life on the road, her ability to rest anywhere shouldn't have surprised him.

What surprised him was that she'd been able to shut out the events of the evening long enough for her sleep mechanism to kick in and her subconscious to take over. The mind's defense system was an amazing thing.

Not long after she'd drifted off, he'd eased out from under her and examined Cowboy, then caught a catnap or two in Doc Harmon's office chair, resetting his internal alarm every couple of hours, rechecking Cowboy's blood count each time.

Standing in the treatment room listening to the dog breathe, Tyler checked the clock on the wall and weighed his options. Five o'clock. Doc Harmon wasn't due in for at least four hours, if he came in at all before rounds.

His receptionist, Annette, doubled as a technician, and usually opened the clinic around eight-thirty. Tyler knew she'd assisted the doctor in surgery. But he didn't want to wait the forty minutes or more it would take her to make the drive in from the northernmost corner of the county.

He didn't have a problem going in alone, but as weak as the dog was, he preferred to have an assistant watch the monitors.

When he heard a heavy truck roll past the back door, he thought he might have found his man.

Stepping out into the predawn gloom, Tyler watched while Rico pulled DayLine's one-ton pickup to a stop in front of the new hospital. The big Latino cut the engine, easily stepped down from the high cab and slammed the door.

At seeing Tyler, Rico lifted his chin in greeting. "How's Sophie?"

Tyler motioned toward the clinic with a turn of his head. "Still asleep."

Rico nodded. "And the dog?"

"So-so." He sighed, rubbed at the base of his neck. "I've gotta go in. You up to assisting?"

Rico took a minute to think, then made a disgusted face and said, "As long as I don't have to see blood or touch guts."

Tyler grinned. "I'll handle the blood and guts. I just need you to watch the heart monitor. Check his gums once in a while and make sure they stay pinked up."

"Sounds clean enough."

"I'd like to get it done before Sophie wakes up. I'd like to be able to give her a little good news."

Rico's long, quiet stride brought him closer. He lowered his voice. "*Dios.* So it's not so good right now?"

"It could be a lot better."

He blew out a low whistle, shook his head. "That dog is all she's got, man. This father thing...I've got my own theories about how that's gonna turn out. But I know exactly what's gonna happen if Sophie loses that dog."

As interested as he was in Rico's theories, Tyler didn't have time. "Which is why I'm gonna do the Super Vet thing and make sure she doesn't."

Rico took a long moment to consider Tyler's expression. His eyes narrowed. "Then these hours you're keeping here aren't just for the dog?"

Tyler lifted a shoulder, wondering why weighty admissions seemed easy to make in the dark. And why he wasn't the least bit uncomfortable admitting it to this man. "What can I say?"

Rico moved forward, met Tyler eye-to-eye. "You can say you care about her, man."

"I can do better than that."

"*Bueno. Muy bueno,*" he said, clamping his hand down on Tyler's shoulder in friendly counsel. "Then I won't worry so much about her staying behind."

"You don't have to worry at all," Tyler said, meeting the Latino's challenge head-on.

Rico's face broke into a huge grin. "Ah, glad to hear it, *mi amigo*. Now that that's settled, why don't we quit wasting time?"

THE TREATMENT ROOM and surgery suite smelled of disinfectant and a bitter-tasting mixture of fluids and drugs.

The odors weren't a big deal to Tyler but, figuring Rico and Sophie might think the place smelled like a morgue, he pushed the exhaust vent wide open then turned back to the task at hand.

When he looked up from adjusting Cowboy's IV, he found Sophie standing in the doorway, her clothes wrinkled, her hair a ragged mess. But her physical appearance registered only peripherally.

What registered was the way she scrunched her nose at the odors, the way she squinted against the stinging smells, the way bewilderment settled in and then fear, the way her eyes suddenly widened and tears fell and she pressed her fingers to her mouth to hold back the sobs.

Aw, hell. He shook his head, but before he could get out a reassuring word, Rico grabbed a paper towel to dry his hands, turned from the sink and caught sight of her.

"C'mon, *güerita.* No need for those big sad eyes. The doc's been in here working magic."

Tyler closed the door to the ICU pen, crossed the room and dropped a kiss on her forehead. "He had a ruptured spleen, Sophie. I've given him a transfusion to replace the blood he lost. As long as the chest drain does its thing, his lungs and ribs heal up and infection doesn't set in, he should be fine."

She closed her eyes and sagged against him. "Are you sure?"

He had to be honest because false hope was no hope at all. "As sure as I can be about anything at this stage of the game."

She crossed the room to the ICU pen, ran a palm down the cage door then slipped two fingers through the wire mesh and slowly stroked Cowboy's ear. The dog lifted his tail in one weak wag and Sophie smiled through her tears. She leaned down and spoke to him quietly, then stood and tucked her hands into her front pockets.

Tyler followed slowly and stood off to the side, watching as her gaze roamed over her dog, listening as her breathing settled into the same pattern as Cowboy's, sensing as much as seeing the slow crawl of relief into her features.

His gut knotted. He hadn't even been close in his estimation of what this dog meant to her. Of the responsibility he'd taken on. Of how much trust Sophie had placed in his hands. *Aw, hell.*

Turning at an angle to the pen, she blinked to clear the moisture from her eyes and looked first at him then at Rico as if they were the two most important men in her life. "Thank you."

Then she hiccuped. The hiccup turned into a laugh. Then a giggle. And when a silly grin spread over her face it was all Tyler could do to keep his hands to himself.

"Can we go get some breakfast?" Her grin widened. "I'm starving."

She had to be one of a kind. And it was a damn good thing she was going to be his. "Sounds good to me. As long as we can get it to go. I'm feeling a little bit skanky right now."

She frowned as if finally noticing the splotches staining his jeans and the front of his long-sleeved pullover T-shirt. "You look like you just saved my dog's life. And mine. So, I'm buying. And no arguments from either of you."

Rico glanced at Tyler. His expression resembled one of gastric pain. "You know what she eats."

"Yeah." Tyler cut her a private glance. "I know what she eats."

"C'mon, guys," she pleaded. "This is a special occasion. I want pancakes drizzled with butter and syrup."

Rico laughed. "You two go ahead. I've got to check on the crew." He sobered. "We're pulling out, Sophie."

Her smile faded as she hunched her shoulders forward protectively. "You know I can't go."

"I know. I'll get in touch with you through the doc, say, in a week or so. See how things are looking here. I'll get the home office to send me a replacement, but I want you back, *güerita*, you hear me?"

"I'll be back, Rico."

Not if he had anything to say about it, Tyler thought as he moved into the surgery suite to cut off the lights. This wasn't the time or place to insist that she wasn't going anywhere, especially as prickly as she got about rights and wrongs.

He stepped back into the treatment room in time to see her give Rico a goodbye hug and toss a playful punch at the Latino's huge biceps.

"I'm going to miss you guys," she said, then amended, "well, at least most of you guys."

Rico headed toward the rear exit, slapping Tyler on the back as he passed. "Take care of my girl, man."

"I'll take care of her. And thanks."

Rico winked and left. Sophie pulled Tyler in the opposite direction, across the treatment room and into the reception area where she impatiently shuffled from foot to foot while he called in their breakfast order to Ford's.

Once he locked up the clinic and they reached the truck, he opened the driver's side door. Sophie clambered up inside and nearly bounced off the ceiling. She even patted the seat in a "hurry up" motion.

Tyler rolled his eyes and climbed in beside her. This adrenaline rush was out of control and she was gonna be feeling it soon. He needed to get her fed and get her home before she crashed.

He pulled out of the parking lot and headed for Ford's Diner. "What's the rush?"

"I haven't eaten since lunch yesterday. I'm starving. And I want to hurry so I can get back to Cowboy."

"Sounds like critical hunger to me. There's a couple dozen cookies there on the seat beside you if you're desperate."

"Cookies?" She cast a quick glance at the plastic container then cut her gaze back to him. "A little stash of home cooking for later?"

"What can I say?"

"You can say we're almost there."

"We're there. I'm going in to pick up the food. But after that we're both going home." He pulled into Ford's parking lot, put the truck in Park, got out and looked back. "Now don't be doing that lip thing, Sophie North. I haven't slept. I need a shower. And Doc Harmon's on his way in."

"But I can't. Something might happen."

"And if something happens the doc will know what to do. He's been taking care of Brodie County's animals longer than you or I have been alive. And unlike me he's not real fond of hovering owners.

"Besides," he said, backing away from the open door

and Sophie's growing exasperation, "once you get a bellyful of pancakes, I want you rested up because we've got a party tonight."

By the time he returned, hands full with two foam boxes and a bag of plastic ware, she was fuming.

"I hope you're kidding about the party," she said, snatching the food from his hands.

"Nope." He backed the truck out of the parking lot and headed out to the county highway. "But to tell you the truth the date had slipped my mind until I called for the pancakes and Rachel reminded me."

"Who's the party for?" she asked warily around her first bite.

"Well, actually it's for me."

Her eyes widened incredulously. "And you forgot about it?"

"I didn't forget the party, I just forgot it was tonight, what with all that happened yesterday." He looked down at the rapidly dwindling breakfast. Both breakfasts. "Hey, how 'bout saving some of that for me?"

"Is it your birthday?" she asked, and fed him a bite.

He chewed and swallowed before answering. "No. It's a combination house warming and grand opening. Harley's in charge, which means attendance is mandatory."

She looked down, swirled the plastic fork through a puddle of syrup. "I don't think I'm in the mood for a party."

"I'm not exactly up for it, either, but we're both going to go. I owe it to Harley for all the work she's done, and you need a break."

"But, Cowboy—"

"Cowboy will be fine. He doesn't need to sense you there worrying about him. Now c'mon. You can sleep for a while before putting on your party clothes. I'll come get you early and we'll drop by the clinic before we head out to my house."

"The party's at your new house?"

"Yeah, and I've got to show you the tub in the master bath. I swear Gardner's out of his mind. It's a pool. Big enough to swim laps in."

She fed him another bite then finished his pancakes while no doubt thinking up a list of excuses.

"I can't go. I don't have any party clothes with me."

Well, now, he hadn't thought of that one. "I tell you what. We'll go by Camelot first. Harley's a bit taller than you but I'm sure she can fix you right up."

"Are you saying I need to be fixed up?"

"No. I'm saying that Harley would love to get her hands on you just like she did with Gardner and me and Jud. It'll be fun. Trust me."

"Do I have a choice?"

"Not a one." He pulled up in front of the cabin. After putting the truck in Park, he took both empty pancake boxes from her hands and tossed them on the floorboard. Then he reached behind her and knocked the plastic container of cookies to the floor, as well.

She looked from the floor to his face. "You don't want those?"

"I want you," he said, and shamelessly took her mouth.

He couldn't remember need ever being this strong before, didn't know what he had done in his life before Sophie, wanted to crush her determination to leave.

And so he laid her back on the seat, one hand cradling her head, the other palm sliding from her throat to her breast to her belly to her hip. He claimed her, let her know with his hands and his mouth that this time he wasn't going to let her get away.

Then he raised his head and said it. "I'm not thrilled with the way this second chance came about, but I'm not about to waste it or be so subtle this time.

"I love you, Sophie. I want you to think about that for a while today. I want you to try it on. See how it fits in with your plans."

Then he sat up, pulled her up with him and opened the truck door. He hauled her out, guided her to the cabin steps and left her there in a daze.

SOPHIE STOOD in the doorway of the cabin wearing her tan work boots, a pair of blue jeans and a white T-shirt. This T-shirt had long sleeves and a daringly scooped and scalloped neckline. It was as frilly as she got.

Tyler's insistence that his sister-in-law could solve her clothing problem led Sophie to believe that she and Harley might be close to the same size.

If not, well, there were always safety pins. With the tricks she'd learned through the years, she shouldn't have a bit of trouble adjusting a skirt to fit.

Safety pins wouldn't be much help when it came to shoes, however. And Sophie traveled with minimum footwear—the work boots she was wearing now, and a pair of black and white leather hi-top athletic shoes. Neither of which went with a skirt and a scooped and scalloped long-sleeved white T-shirt.

Of course, worrying about clothes and shoes and parties was ridiculous when what she should be worrying about was what she was going to say to the man who was on his way to pick her up. The man she'd been thinking about all afternoon.

The man who'd told her he loved her.

The kiss he'd given her when he'd dropped her at the cabin was the first physical move he'd made since the morning after that one incredible night.

Since then, they'd forged a bond of friendship, a bond she knew was important because it encompassed her needs in a healthy combination of respect, care and concern.

The only relationship requirement absent from her list was a warm, cozy, safe attraction. Instead what they had was a wondrous heat, a steadily growing fire fed by conversation and tender touches and long, lingering looks.

The temptation of Tyler was more than lust, and the knowledge frightened her. Frightened her enough to make her realize it was time to stop judging her future by her past. To find out the truth about rights and wrongs and chances.

And while she was searching, she would do her best to figure out why, in the long hours spent today deciding to explore this thing with Tyler, she hadn't once considered how her decision would affect her search for her father.

At the sound of tires clattering over the new bridge, Sophie looked up. Tyler's sexy red truck moved closer, the tinted windows obscuring all but the vaguest outline of his head and the shape of his shoulders. But that vague outline was enough.

Her stomach fluttered deep behind her ribs. Her palms began to sweat; she wiped them on the seat of her jeans, realizing as she did that she held her lower body taut to fight the tingling and emptiness in her belly.

She closed her eyes then and let it happen, testing, feeling, experiencing what she'd refused to embrace in the past. This uncontrollable physical response was what she'd cut herself off from, what she'd assigned to the type of person she refused to become.

But tonight she was happy. This feeling was all for Tyler, because of Tyler. He'd told her that he loved her, so she let her body take her away.

The truck rolled to a stop. He left it running, stepped down and headed toward her, his black fringed lace-up boots polished, his dark blue Wranglers pressed, his silver belt buckle laying low beneath his waist. He wore a button-down shirt striped in blues and tans, and a casually cut brown sportcoat.

His hair picked up light from the afternoon sun and lay in that perfect cut that she'd admired the first day she'd seen him. It had grown long over the past six weeks, the ends hanging below his collar. But the cut was made to last, and when he brushed it off his forehead, the strands settled in a sexy disarray.

He'd reached her now and his eyes were bright, the green the color of all outdoors. His gaze took in her hair then moved lower, to her eyes, her lips, stopping at her throat where her pulse beat like crazy. His lids grew heavy, his pupils darkened with arousal.

He raised a hand, ran a finger along her neckline, the rough pad of his finger a slide of sensation tickling her collarbone and the swell of her unbound breasts.

Her nipples peaked against the cotton of her T-shirt, and a shudder had her closing her eyes, had her body straining, swaying, seeking his.

He moved his hand to cup her nape then fingered the tiny diamond studs—a graduation present to herself—she'd slipped in her lobes. She looked up in time to see him smile, and the big bad wolf grin that spread over his face left her unable to breathe.

"You look good enough to eat."

So do you, she silently answered, but said aloud, "If your sister-in-law doesn't have anything I can wear, I'm not going to this party."

"Yes, you are." His finger returned to her neckline, dipped low into her cleavage, teased her into a long slow moan. "You've dressed up those blue jeans just fine, darlin'."

He was obviously blinded by the love he'd claimed. And after that moan, she could only hope he'd been struck deaf, as well. She shifted uncomfortably, dislodging his hand. "Can we go? I'd really like to check in on Cowboy."

"I spoke with Doc Harmon before leaving Camelot," Tyler said, taking her elbow and guiding her down off the porch. "Cowboy's sleeping fine. His blood count looks better. His breathing and his pulse are stable."

"So he's going to be okay?"

"It's looking good."

She jumped into the truck seat and stayed in the middle because it seemed to be where she belonged.

With the belonging came that weird sense of homesickness, that crazy feeling that she shouldn't be feeling because this thing with Tyler had nothing to do with home.

Did it?

Sophie pursed her lips. Maybe that was another feeling she needed to test. Maybe she was searching for home and family in the wrong place.

Second chances were too few and far between, though, so she was determined to discover the truth. After all, being wrong wasn't such a bad thing.

Was it?

CAMELOT'S MAIN HOUSE was a Western fantasy. Standing in the open doorway of Tyler's truck, Sophie stared up at the two-story, white, frame house with lust in her heart. A covered porch ran the length of the front and along two sides, and barn-red shutters flanked every window.

Miniature rosebushes, in artfully tended and protected winter beds, huddled close to the house, while the climbing variety lived up to their name, scaling the sections of trellis that formed a privacy screen between the porch floor and overhanging roof.

Sophie took a huge breath and remembered all the reasons she shouldn't be here. This was a home like she'd never had, this was where Tyler had grown up. How much different could beginnings, ways of life, expectations get?

On the drive in she'd nearly drooled over the grounds, the barns and corrals and pastures spread out over acres of property. The cars and trucks and more trucks. The redwood deck and in-ground pool fenced off behind the house. The wooden swing set and jungle gym tucked protectively near the back door.

What was she doing here?

Why had she bothered with the earrings or the extra fluff she'd given her hair? She was so out of her league.

"C'mon, Prickle Puss," Tyler teased, taking hold of her hand to tug her away from his truck.

She pulled her hand from his, crossed her arms over her chest, dug her heels in deep. "I shouldn't be here. I can't be here. I've changed my mind. Take me back."

A screen door whacked shut and Tyler said, "Too late."

He stepped behind her, forced her away from the truck and locked the door, smugly bouncing the keys in his palm before shoving them deep into his pocket.

She mimicked his self-satisfied smirk, gave up all attempt to stand her ground and surrendered to his determined forward motion. And when she looked toward the porch she knew without a doubt that the woman standing on the top step holding a baby in the crook of one arm was Harley.

She wore black lace-up half boots, black leggings and a long-sleeve, oversize white tuxedo shirt. The cool wind whipped through blond hair that tumbled to her shoulders and her blue eyes shone like the bright winter sky. She looked completely out of her element, yet totally at home, and Sophie marginally relaxed.

Harley's gaze followed their progress up the steps, skipping briefly over Tyler before scanning Sophie from head to toe and back again. A secretive smile pulled at her lips and her expression settled into one of pure female satisfaction.

She didn't even wait for Tyler to make introductions. "Ah, Sophie. So, you're what's wrong with my brother-in-law."

"Actually, he was already like this when I met him,"

Sophie said, and when Harley laughed in response that homesick feeling settled in to stay.

"Very funny, both of you," Tyler said, following Sophie up the front steps. He tugged teasingly at a strand of her hair. "You I forgive because you were led astray. But you," he said, pointing to Harley, "can wipe that silly grin off your face."

"No, way," Harley said, and increased the power of her smile. "I've waited for this moment far too long. I'm not about to give up this front row center seat."

"Pay no attention to my sister-in-law," Tyler instructed Sophie, tossing a warning glance Harley's way. "Her sense of humor is suffering from birth. Or should I say, her sense of humor has been suffering *since* birth."

Harley shifted the baby to her shoulder, settled the blanket around the tiny fuzz-covered head and, sending a playful wink in Sophie's direction, breezed past Tyler on into the house.

"I wouldn't be making jokes if I were you, Doctor D. Not unless you can take the heat as well as you dish it out," she called over her shoulder.

Sophie was enchanted. The banter between the two adults was so fresh and so perfect and so rare in her experience, where family exchanges had leaned toward snide and vulgar.

She followed Harley inside and when Harley stopped, she moved up behind, taking a minute to stroke a knuckle over the baby's soft cheek, gently caress the soft downy head and tiny fingers that rested on Harley's shoulder.

"She's beautiful," Sophie whispered. The dark gray-blue eyes focused on her face, the wee hand latched on to her own, tugging on her heart as surely as it tugged on her finger. She shut her eyes briefly and hugged the sensation close, letting it wrap her securely in its tender hold.

Oh, God, this was what she wanted, what she'd been missing all her life, what she'd spent years searching for, seeking, longing to discover, hoping when she finally found her father the magic would follow.

But standing here, tiny eyes studying her own, miniature fingers wrapped around one of hers, listening to Tyler and Harley's teasing exchange, she felt for all the world as if her future had been defined in this moment.

Because this was the magic, this feeling of warmth and affection growing deep within, this sense of belonging and acceptance, this silent invitation to be a part of the joy. And she finally realized, for the first time she truly understood, that the bond of blood played only a part in creating a family's love.

Harley craned her neck to watch the baby root at Sophie's finger. "I've got to get this kid fed before I spring a leak."

"Aw, Harley," Tyler whined, closing the door behind him. "Don't be talking about all that female stuff."

She motioned Sophie forward. "My brother-in-law. He can pull a calf without thinking twice but he gags at the idea of breast milk."

Sophie drew in a deep, steadying breath and followed Harley farther into the house. She was halfway across a comfortable living room full of male power furniture and livable antiques before she realized Tyler was still standing at the door.

She looked from his pained expression to Harley and back. "Tyler?"

Harley stopped and turned around, took in her brother-in-law's dazed appearance and rolled her eyes. She leaned forward and whispered to Sophie, "It was the breast milk that did it. Men. They love sex. But you mention reproduction and they go into huge apoplectic fits.

"Yoo-hoo, Tyler?" She waved her hand. "Gardner and the boys are in the barn with the new colt. Why don't you head down there and let Sophie and me get acquainted?"

Tyler pushed away from the front door and headed toward the kitchen. When Sophie would have accompanied him into the spacious spick-and-span room, Harley stopped her at the doorway and directed her toward the foot of the stairs. "We'll go upstairs to visit while I feed Dani so I won't have to worry about offending anyone's delicate sensibilities."

"You know, Harley," Tyler began, shaking his head, "I don't remember what I did in my life for hard times before you came along to give them to me."

"And it's always been my pleasure," Harley replied.

"Oh, I don't have a doubt about that." Tyler pushed open the door to what looked to be a washroom set off the back porch. "Listen, I told Sophie you might be able to help her out with clothes for the party."

"You know me well, brother-in-law. I'd love to," Harley answered.

"Great. And if either of you is looking to make fun of me any more—" he jerked a thumb that direction "—I'll be out in the barn with the boys."

"Good, because we have girl things to do," Harley said, taking hold of Sophie's hand and pulling her up the staircase. "Oh, Tyler. Are your keys in the truck?"

"I have them right here," he said, digging into his pocket.

"Toss them on the table, will ya? Sophie and I are gonna go get gorgeous. You can ride down to the Animal Kingdom with Gardner and the boys and we'll follow later in your truck. Just tell that husband of mine to leave Dani's car seat on the porch."

Tyler shook his head and grinned at Sophie. "What did I tell you?" he asked, then headed out the back door.

"What did he tell you about what?" Harley asked, leading the way up the stairs.

Sophie chose her words carefully. She didn't want to blow the beginnings of what looked to be a very special friendship. "Just that you were a very in-charge woman. It was all complimentary."

"Oh, I'm sure it was. And, even if it wasn't, I'm not about to apologize for having a firm touch. You try living on a ranch with eight full-time hands, two grown men and their uncle and now four children."

"I'm impressed already," Sophie said. They'd reached the top of the stairs and headed down the hall. "Uh, what's the Animal Kingdom?"

"That's what the boys, Austin, Ben and Cody, have nicknamed their uncle's house. They also call him Doctor Doolittle, but I try not to rub that one in."

Ah, that explained the Doctor D, Sophie thought, tucking away the ammunition.

Harley led her to a bedroom at the end of the hall, a

room done in tones of dark green and peach, heavy wood pieces and feminine accents in florals and lace. Obviously the room she shared with Gardner. And just as obviously a room she was comfortable showing to strangers.

With the baby settled safely on her stomach in the center of the king-size bed, Harley pulled open an incredible walk-in closet. "Let's see," she said, whipping through the hangers on one side. "You're a bit shorter than I am. And I'd say you were, what? A six?"

"No. Too many muscles."

"An eight then, which is still reason enough to hate you." Harley poked her head around the closet door and smiled. "Most of my things are tens, but we'll figure something out."

"How dressy is the party?" Sophie asked, perching delicately on the end of the bed, her fingers curled into the blanket on either side of her hips. She couldn't imagine what it must be like to sleep in the same bed every night.

"It's not dressy at all." Harley had returned to the depths of the closet. "In fact, what you're wearing would work just fine. But I have a feeling that brother-in-law of mine is itching to see a different you." She reappeared, hangers caught in one hand. "And I think you might like that, too."

"I told him this was a crazy idea. I don't pack for parties when I'm on the road." Not that she owned party clothes anyway. "But you're probably right about him being tired of seeing me in jeans since that's all he's seen me in."

"Oh, I don't think tired is the word." Harley tossed

the clear protective bags to the floor and hung three items over the top of the closet's open door then disappeared back inside. "As a matter of fact, I can't remember ever seeing him that close to having his eyeballs pop out of his head."

Thank goodness Harley couldn't see the flush spreading up Sophie's neck. "I thought that was because of the breast milk."

"He might have been disgusted with that, but I was talking about before and after." She reappeared again, hung four more items on the door. "I'm talking about the way his eyes eat you up like a starving man. I have experience with a starving man. I know what I'm talking about."

Harley finished her forage into the closet and plopped down beside Sophie on the bed. "Well? What are you waiting for?"

Sophie didn't know what she was waiting for because she didn't even know what she was doing. The closet. The clothes. She was supposed to try on clothes. But all she could think about was a big bad wolf eating her up with his eyes.

"There are two or three dresses there that might work. And several skirt and blouse combinations." Harley placed Dani on her lap, where she began to squirm and fuss in earnest. Harley turned the baby over, patted her back and said to Sophie, "A couple of the skirts might go just as well with the T-shirt you're wearing."

Easing off the mattress, Sophie headed toward the closet, smoothing a hand down her front. "You think this would be okay?"

"Sure. In fact, if it'll make you more comfortable, I'll keep it casual, too."

"Oh, no," Sophie said, standing on one foot to unlace the boot on the other. "You don't have to dress down for me. Just wear what you'd planned to wear."

"I really hadn't planned anything. But, now that I think about it, I have this skirt that drives Gardner insane." The corner of her mouth lifted in a wicked female smile. "It's cut to tie like a sarong and made from the top of an old patchwork quilt. It reminds him of...oh, never mind." She waved her hand. "The matching T-shirt is a wonderful sunflower-yellow silk that's cut very similar to yours...are you all right?"

Sophie dropped boot number two to the floor and shook off the picture of Tyler in white socks and a white shirt and a very thin coverlet. "I'm fine," she managed to squeeze out without moaning. "It's just that I haven't tried on girl clothes in so long that I'm not sure where to start."

"Start with that Indian print skirt. Four pregnancies and I can't wear it anymore. I don't know why I keep it. Except that it was one of the first things Gardner saw me in—and out of."

Sophie carried the hanger into the closet where she slipped out of her jeans. The skirt was gorgeous, the colors bright, the material soft. Yes, she'd try it on but she certainly wouldn't wear it. Not with Gardner sure to be at the party.

She wasn't quite as comfortable with her sexuality as Harley appeared to be. Not that she didn't plan to work on it tonight, just not wearing this particular skirt, even though it looked and felt like a dream once she got it on.

When she stepped into the bedroom to model the skirt for Harley, Sophie found the other woman with the hem of her huge blouse partially raised and her baby nursing contentedly.

Harley glanced up and studied the skirt. "You want to wear that? It looks great."

"I don't think it's really me," Sophie said, slipping out of the skirt and returning it to the hanger.

Harley frowned in concentration. "Maybe something shorter? To show off those great legs?"

"No, I like this length. It's just that—"

"You don't want to wear something that has my memories attached. I understand. And if I could get into it, I'd wear it myself."

"I do like this one, though," Sophie said, pulling a long black column skirt from the closet door.

"Oooh, that might just be the one. You've got the perfect figure for that. And with your light skin and blond hair..." Smiling her approval, Harley let the sentence trail.

The skirt didn't belong on a ranch, that was for sure. It was straight out of a fashion magazine, made from a slinky, sexy, fabric that Sophie knew would feel like heaven—and nothing like blue jeans—on her skin.

And speaking of blue jeans. She glanced the length of Harley's closet. "Your wardrobe surprises me. I guess I thought I'd find..."

"Jeans, jeans and more jeans?" Harley shifted the baby to the other breast. "You know what they say. You can take the girl out of the city, but don't even try to take the city out of the girl."

Sophie lifted the skirt from the hanger and stepped into the closet. "How long have you lived here?"

"Ten years. Don't get me wrong. I wouldn't live any-place else. But those clothes...that's who I am. I was thirty when I married Gardner. I've given him four children in ten years and a lot of myself in the process. But there's still a big part of me that doesn't belong to Camelot."

Sophie closed her eyes as the skirt shimmied down over her hips. Once it settled above her ankles, she returned to the bedroom. "It wasn't hard to give up your other life?"

"It was one of the hardest things I've ever done. But I don't regret a minute of my life." Harley stroked a finger over the baby's cheek, then looked up. Her face filled with delight. "Oh, my God, that is so perfect on you. Just perfect.

"Listen, I know it's chilly out, but if you can stand it there's a pair of platform sandals that would be to die for with that skirt." Her eyes suddenly widened. "Oh, oh, what am I thinking? In the back of the closet there's a sweater chest. Second drawer. Grab the black cashmere."

Sophie found the shoes on the rack in the closet and the sweater in the drawer. The shoes were a half size off but close enough. The sweater, on the other hand, was perfect, loose enough that she wouldn't have to worry about her lack of a bra and as soft as a caress on her skin.

She came back out for Harley's inspection and whoop of, "Oh, this is so great. Tyler is just going to die."

"You think so?"

"I definitely think so. Come see for yourself," she said, motioning Sophie toward the full-length mirror standing in the corner of the room.

Sophie moved to check her reflection. The sleeves of the sweater were long, the neckline loosely woven, showing the line of her collarbone, the swell of her breasts, and giving a hint of frill to the sweep of plain black. The hem hit her mid-torso, leaving a good two inches of skin and her navel exposed above the waistband of the skirt.

Except the skirt had no waistband, only a small turned-under hem, a zipper and a walking slit in back. It hung on her hip bones, fell in a long straight line from there to the floor. When she walked, the material moved with her, clinging to her thighs and her long slope of hip.

The length of her own legs amazed her. As did the curves outlined so clearly beneath all that black. Harley had been right. The contrast between the clothing and Sophie's skin and hair brought out the green in her eyes, the flush in her cheeks and color in her lips, and shadowed the skin of her belly.

The woman in the mirror couldn't be her. She wasn't so intriguing, so confident in her bearing, so comfortable with her femininity, so...so...provocative and sexy.

Was this who Tyler saw when he looked at her?

She took a deep breath. "Well, I don't exactly want Tyler to die."

"No, I don't guess you do. But it's fun to see them sweat, you know."

Sophie turned then, twisted her hands at her waist

and, hiking the tight skirt up her thighs, sat next to Harley on the edge of the bed. "No. I don't know. I haven't dated much."

"Honey, from the look in my brother-in-law's eyes you're not going to be dating again anytime soon," Harley said, wrapping one arm around Sophie's shoulder in a girlfriend hug.

"This thing with Tyler...I just don't have any idea what happened."

"It hit you fast and it hit you hard, didn't it?"

"But I don't know what it was that hit me."

Harley adjusted her clothing and lay the sleeping baby behind her in the center of the bed. She turned to the side, took Sophie's hands in her own. "These Barnes men don't make it easy on us women. They come along right when we've figured out what we want and where we're going, and make us wonder what we're doing with our lives. It just doesn't seem fair that a man should have that much power, does it?"

Sophie shook her head, looked up and met Harley's compassionate gaze.

"Then do what I do," Harley said, "and don't ever let him know. Instead, enjoy every single moment of the power you hold over him."

The first part she'd figured out on her own. Tyler's upper hand was already too high. But the second... "The thing is, I was due to leave yesterday. My crew pulled out today in fact. But my dog was hurt and I had to stay."

"And you don't know who you stayed behind for. Tyler or your dog."

No, she knew that, didn't she? If Cowboy hadn't been

hurt she would've left with the crew yesterday. She would have. She knew that.

But Tyler had said he loved her and now she was the one whose mind was mush. *Rats.*

HOW HE COULD HEAR the front door open and close above the din of party-goers, Tyler wasn't sure. But he could and he did and every time the new arrival wasn't Sophie the muscle in his jaw clenched tighter. An hour into the party and he was working on a hell of a headache.

The first floor of the custom log home consisted of a large open area. A two-way stone fireplace built across the width partitioned one third of the huge room into an island kitchen and dining alcove where the women of Brodie County had put on some kind of feed.

Card tables set end to end held foil-lined platters of smoked meats, crockery bowls brimming with vegetables and salads, sugar-headed meringue pies, trays of kid-tempting, palm-size cookies and red plastic tumblers filled with drinks.

Rachel and Mrs. Ford supervised the food line, directing guests through the kitchen and into the living room where more card tables and folding chairs sat in cozy clusters. A few visitors chose to take Tyler's tour before eating, following him up the staircase at the far end of the room.

After a quick look around the second floor's four empty bedrooms and two baths, he led them back down to the master suite that occupied the house's only separate wing. Privacy in a master suite was a good thing. Would *be* a good thing, Tyler mused, disgruntled.

But he'd just come from *his* bedroom and right now there had to be twenty people checking out *his* tub, another ten in *his* closet. And now, here, another fifty milled through the main living area.

Yet the one person he most wanted to see hadn't arrived. He was going to throttle Harley if she didn't get Sophie here soon.

When Harley planned a party, she planned a party and unfortunately she'd planned this one before Sophie had come along. So, along with the invitations, Harley had dropped a lot of well-placed hints about her brother-in-law's status as eligible bachelor.

Which meant every mother of every eligible Brodie County daughter hovered, refilling his plate with baked beans and potato salad, barbecued brisket and homemade rolls.

He had already ducked out and loosened his belt a notch and he'd only been here an hour. If he didn't stop eating now and walk off the food laying heavy in his stomach, he'd fall asleep before Sophie got here. And that couldn't happen.

He had plans for the end of the evening, plans he intended to carry out while wide, wide awake.

"Hey, Uncle Ty."

Tyler turned at the sound of his oldest nephew's voice. "Austin, buddy. What's up?"

Dressed in crisp blue jeans, boots and a wildly colored shirt, Austin pointed back toward Tyler's bedroom. "I was just in your bathroom with Daddy."

Tyler arched a brow. "Oh, yeah? He didn't leave the seat up again, did he?"

Austin giggled, then quickly stopped because he was nine and nine-year-olds weren't supposed to giggle anymore. "No, Uncle Ty. He was telling us that as soon as you move in, that me and Ben and Cody can get Uncle Jud to bring us over for a camp-out and you'll let us have a water balloon fight in the tub."

Tyler ruffled Austin's sandy-blond hair. "Your daddy said that, did he?"

"Yeah, but I gotta go now cuz there's almost no chocolate chip cookies left and I've only had six." Austin scrambled away.

Tyler watched him go. *Kids.* He wondered how Sophie felt about becoming a parent, because he didn't think life would be quite as much fun without a couple of the monsters turning his world upside down.

He cast another glance at the front door and found his brother heading toward him. Once Gardner was within hearing distance, Tyler pinned him down. "Camp-outs and water balloon fights?"

Gardner grinned. "You've been talking to Austin."

"I knew you had ulterior motives for building me this house, but just to get your wife alone? That's low, Gardner. Really low. Snake-belly low."

Hands on his hips, Gardner hung his head and grinned. "What can I say? Harley and I haven't had a night alone in that house since...well, since never."

"What did you expect? You didn't just bring her home, you brought her home to eight ranch hands and two live-in relatives. Next time you get married, why don't you build a house for your wife instead of your brother?"

"There's not going to be a next time, little brother, which is why you'll do the right thing and take my family off my hands from time to time." Gardner glanced around the room and frowned. "Speaking of family, what have you done with my wife and your woman?"

His woman. He liked the caveman sound of that. "I left them upstairs at Camelot trying on clothes."

"Well, that could take well into the next century," Gardner groused, turning his head at the sound of the front door opening. "But then again, maybe not."

Tyler followed Gardner's lead. He took in the picture of Sophie walking through his door and knew this was one of those moments that came too seldom in a lifetime. One of those moments that took hold of a man's soul, reminding him he was only human and easily brought to his knees.

"Is that some piece of work or what?" Gardner asked, whistling under his breath.

"Yeah. She is," Tyler answered, having eyes for no one but Sophie. What the hell was she doing living her life in worn boots and jeans?

She wore nothing but black and it took him about half a second to decide it was his favorite color. Especially considering the way the slinky fabric molded and shaped her long arms and legs, clung to breasts he knew fit his hands, and caressed hips he vowed would soon cradle his own.

Her eyes were bright, the color high in her cheeks, and her hair had the tousled look of a man's impatient hands. As if that tempting sweep of shoulder-to-shoulder skin wasn't enough to light his fire, he swore there was a good hand span of belly showing between her sweater and her skirt.

He knew exactly how incredible her body was, but to see her wearing purely female clothes left his tongue fighting the wad of cotton his mouth had become. He couldn't speak. Hell, he couldn't even swallow.

He turned to Gardner and decided his brother's knocked-for-a-loop expression must have mirrored his own.

Gardner pulled his gaze from Harley, who was no less stunning than Sophie in a short, figure-hugging skirt and bright yellow blouse, and grinned like a devil at Tyler. "You look like you just swallowed a tumbleweed."

Tyler cleared his throat. "And here I thought it was a hay bale."

Gardner affectionately gripped Tyler's upper arm and glanced from Tyler to the doorway and back again. His grin widened. "You know, little brother, this isn't going to go away."

"Goddamn, I hope not," Tyler said under his breath, his heart in his throat, a saddle cinch tight around his chest. "Just tell me it's not going to kill me."

"Not right away. But over time? Yeah, I'd say you're a definite goner." Gardner slipped his arm around Tyler's shoulder in a gesture of shared commiseration. "Speaking from experience, though, it's a hell of a way to go."

Tyler was absolutely ready to find out. He grinned, then grew thoughtful. "Hey, if I hadn't made you see the error of your ways, would you have shaped up enough to go after Harley?"

"Taking credit where credit's not due again?"

"Just wondering about life. And chances."

"I don't have to wonder. I know."

"Well?" Tyler prompted, watching emotions flicker like broken light over his brother's face.

"If I hadn't, I'd've been one son of a bitch to live with."

"Hell, you already are," Tyler said, and turned to go get Sophie.

By the time he made it to the entryway, she and Harley had been swallowed by the crowd. Needing a drink to cool his throat, he headed for the kitchen, which for the moment was empty, thank goodness. He drained a glass of water and set it on the counter, then braced his hands on the lip of the sink. Hanging his head, he breathed slowly, deeply, letting his arousal subside.

When he turned, he found Tamara Shotweiler leaning an elbow on the counter, her palomino mane of hair artfully draped over one shoulder so as not to spoil the deep cleavage staring him in the face.

"You look like a man in pain, Tyler Barnes."

He straightened. "Tam. It's been a long time."

"Too long, from that look on your face." She'd turned her back to the counter, braced her weight on both elbows. Her legs were long in turquoise jeans, her feet crossed at the ankle in expensive ostrich-skin boots. Tyler figured her vest was custom-made to draw attention to her spectacular figure.

Funny. She didn't phase him a bit.

"I think that expression you saw was me wondering if I'm ever going to get the Kool-Aid off this floor."

"Nice try, Ty. But we go back a long way. I've seen that look before." She cocked her chin just so. "I know exactly what it means."

He turned up a corner of his mouth. "Well, you got me there."

"So, am I right?" she asked, and shifted her shoulders back farther.

She was really a nice girl. He wondered what had happened to make her think she had to try this hard. "You're right. I just watched the woman I'm going to marry walk into the room and damn if I'm not still feeling it."

Her face darkened. "I didn't know this was an engagement party, too."

"We're not officially engaged," he admitted. No need to put Sophie on the hot seat. "But I do plan to make her my wife."

"I wish you luck, then. Just wish I hadn't waited so long to come home."

There was a long story behind her confession. He'd always been a pretty good listener. "What made you decide to come back, Tam? Last I heard you'd just returned from a European honeymoon and had set up housekeeping in Bel Air."

"What can I say? I missed the West Texas heat."

"Try again."

She shook her head and straightened, brushed her hair back over her shoulder. Her smile was sad. "Not this time. You get back to your party. I think I hear Jim Beam calling my name."

He started to go after her, but caught sight of Lindy Coltrain waving him into the living room. He managed to snag a glimpse of Sophie's back as Harley led her toward the master bedroom, no doubt to show off his tub.

He'd catch up with her in a minute, after he'd dealt with Lindy. If he ever got to Lindy, he thought, waylaid by a half-dozen old friends wishing him well in his new practice. After sending one of his old high school running mates to check on Tamara, he finally reached Lindy.

She cocked her head of red curls to one side and let one brow gradually lift. "I was wondering if I was going to get a chance to see you tonight. Or if you were going to stand me up again."

They'd been friends too long for him to take offense. "C'mon, Lindy. You're not giving me points for good intentions."

"Good intentions, huh? Isn't that where the road to hell comes into play?" she asked, her blue eyes twinkling.

He rocked back on his heels, glanced down at the toes of his boots and, before he could find a quick comeback, she'd linked her arm through his, holding him closer than he wanted to be held by anyone but Sophie.

"I'm just giving you a hard time, Ty. That storm caught more than a few folks off guard. And I caught a whiff of Dad and Lucas after they got home from working on the bridge out to Grandpa's old place. Phew. If you were half as disgusting as they were, I'm glad you decided not to show up."

"Well, I wasn't quite as waterlogged as your dad or your brother. But it was a long day and I wasn't fit company for anyone by the end of it," he said, grimacing as he remembered the way he'd snapped at Sophie.

"So, how about it? Third time's a charm? We could head out to Bo Star's Dance Hall. Kick up our heels. Burn off some of the energy that's keeping you so tense." She squeezed at his upper arm.

He caught sight of Sophie then as Harley herded her into the center of a group of women. Their eyes connected and he lifted his brows and his shoulders in apology.

"I don't think so, Lindy," he said. "My dance card's full."

Lindy slowly released her hold. He looked down to see that she'd followed his gaze to Sophie. Her cute-as-a-button freckled nose turned up in disappointment.

"Well, dang," she said, smiling up at Tyler. "There go my chances of snagging a rich doctor."

Tyler couldn't help but laugh at her generous spirit. "If you want a rich doctor, Lindy, you're looking in the wrong direction."

"Maybe I just changed my mind about doctors period," Lindy said as another of their high school friends walked in the front door. She bounced up and gave Tyler a kiss on the cheek.

"Uh, give my regards to Justin," he said. Lindy ran off and he swore to make her his last distraction. Too late. He'd lost Sophie again.

He looked around the crowded room that was suddenly too crowded for his mood. And as the crowd increased, more friends arriving to wish him the best of luck, his mood darkened further.

He and Sophie had a lot to talk about and he was

tired of waiting to talk. The drive to Camelot from the cabin had taken less than ten minutes. Futures couldn't be settled in such a short span of time.

And since he'd delivered her into Harley's hands, he hadn't seen her except for an occasional too brief glimpse. He wanted to see all of her. To take a really long slow look at what she did to that skirt and blouse and measure that slice of her belly he'd seen.

He made his way through the crowds, wondering if there was anyone in Brodie County not present in the room and if Gardner had built a house this big to make sure Camelot didn't get stuck being the only entertainment capital of the county.

Tyler figured it served him right for being too wrapped up in the hospital plans to check out what his brother was doing. And how it would affect his future.

He laughingly brushed off at least five more come-ons and shook his head in self-amazement. *Man, talk about a change of plans.* It was funny what one blond, green-eyed pixie in the right place at the right time could do to a man.

Now if he could only find her in this madhouse and sneak them both the hell out of here.

10

HE FOUND HER thirty minutes later sitting on the edge of his bathtub, dangling her bare feet over the edge, looking for all the world like she'd just settled in for a long relaxing soak.

The crowd had thinned and she was alone and it was exactly how he wanted her.

"Why don't you turn on the water?"

Dangling her shoes from one finger, she looked up and smiled. "I like it better this way. There's a lot to be said for imagination."

He could only hope their imaginations ran along the same path. "I saw you when you came in."

"I saw you seeing me," she said, running a finger along a ridge on the tub's edge, watching the motion as if fascinated by the slow slide of skin over marble.

He was finding it hard not to lock the door and show her how much better skin could slide over skin when that tub was filled with water. Leaning his backside against the counter, he crossed his ankles and curled his hand around the marble edge. "You seem to have made the rounds tonight."

"You have a lot of friends."

"Yep. Brodie County's just one big happy family."

"I know." She swung around, hiked her skirt and straddled the wide ledge of the tub. The slinky black skirt rode high and left literally nothing to the imagination. Her panties were white.

He shifted, easing one hip onto the counter and releasing a groan in a long spill of breath.

This time she rubbed the marble with long strokes of her palm. Up, then back. Up, then back. "I saw a couple of your friends who looked like they would be more than willing to become permanent family."

He couldn't find his voice to answer. Especially when she swung her other leg over the lip of the tub, crossed one knee over the other. The skirt remained high and her legs were so long and his button fly was killing him.

"I don't think you'll have a bit of trouble becoming engaged by the end of next year." She leaned to the side, one hand splayed on the tub, the other draped over her knee, her sandals dangling from her fingertips.

Slowly, she raised her gaze to his. "But I don't want to talk about that right now."

He wanted to talk about it. He wanted to tell her that he didn't plan to wait until next year to be engaged. In fact, he planned to skip the engagement altogether and elope instead.

But he didn't, because this was a Sophie he hadn't yet seen, soft, and sexily vulnerable and plying her feminine wiles. He could wait. For some things, for talking. He could wait. For other things, he was running out of rein.

He didn't look at her bare feet or her long legs or anywhere but at her face. "Then what is it you want to talk about?"

"Why do we have to talk at all?"

She stood. In one fluid, slow motion. The skirt slid to

her ankles and slowly she crossed the tiled floor. She brushed against him where he stood and he caught her sweet scent in the air, but he didn't move because his heart was pounding, his feet were rooted to the floor and he was afraid that the tiniest motion, a sharp brush of air, the ripple of a spoken word, would shatter the spell.

But then she closed the bathroom door. The latch clicked, the lock snapped and he turned at the command.

She stood with her back to the door, her shoes fallen, forgotten, her arms raised, her hands gripping the wooden clothes' hook over her head. Her chest rose and fell with labored breaths, rapid, audible breaths, and the pulse jumping at the base of her throat pumped to the beat of his blood. Tiny diamond studs twinkled in her lobes when she lifted her chin. Her lower lip trembled but arousal flared wild in her eyes.

"No, we don't have to talk," he managed to get out. His gaze moved from her upraised arms down to her breasts roundly outlined beneath the black fabric to her bare stomach and her toes that curled into the floor. "I can think of a lot of things I'd rather do than talk."

"Then do it," she said. "Kiss me like you haven't since that night on the floor. Kiss me like you love me, Tyler."

Hadn't he always? From that very first time? "Ah, darlin', I thought you'd never ask."

He stepped forward, stopped when only the width of a breath separated their bodies, and cupped her raised elbows in his palms. He slid his hands down the underside of her arms and she trembled. He scooped his thumbs through her armpits down over her breasts and she moaned. Grazed her sides, the bare skin of her belly with his palms, and she whimpered. Then he raised the hem of her sweater to her chin.

Holding her arms high overhead, he teased her nipples with a bare brush of breath, a light sweep of his tongue. Her body shook. She moved to free her hands, but he held her still and let his gaze roam. God, she was beautiful. The faint lighting cast her skin in the color of rich cream, the tips of her breasts in a darker, deeper peach. The sight was sweet and his body was hard, but he still hadn't kissed her.

He didn't trust himself to kiss her the way she'd asked. To kiss her like he loved her would take more time than they had, more privacy than they had, and a softer surface than a wooden door to cushion the strength of his need.

That intensity was exactly what she was expecting, what she feared, so he did his damnedest to grant her request. He brushed his lips over hers with the pure simplicity of a loving kiss, measuring out tiny touches of lips and tongue, gentle nips of teeth.

While his mouth loved her tender, he took her all the way with his hands, shaping her breasts to fit his palms, tugging at her nipples, scraping them with the flat of his hand.

He brushed feather-light kisses along her jaw, pulled her close and reached for the back zipper of her skirt. The material glided to pool around her ankles. He ran his tongue around the shell of her ear, dried the damp trail with warm breath and shoved her panties down to her knees. Then, lifting a boot between her legs, he took the scrap of white to the floor.

He knew she stood naked and knew what she looked like but he kept his eyes closed to keep his kisses sweet and gentle. The rest of him said, To hell with gentle, and hooked her leg around his hip, sliding his arm beneath her thigh until his fingers pressed the heat between her legs.

Her body was wild, yet he held his own still. He kissed her like he loved her, touched her like he loved her, demanding her body accept the truth she was denying in her mind. *This* was what love was, the warm glow as well as the fire.

When she came in his hand, he hushed her tiny whimpers and cries with his mouth. He gentled her, easing her back, letting her body calm. She rested her forehead against his shoulder until her breathing steadied.

Just as she found the strength to look up, to let him see what he swore was love in her eyes, a knock sounded on the door.

"Just a minute," Tyler called as Sophie's eyes went wide and horrified and she scrambled to right her clothes—and find the ones in a heap on the floor.

"Uncle Ty? Is that you?"

Tyler rolled his eyes. "Yeah, Ben-jo. It's me."

"Can I come in? I really gotta go," Tyler's middle nephew murmured, then added more vocally, "Now."

Sophie panicked, her fingers shaking, fumbling with clothing. Tyler shushed her with a finger to her lips and shook his head.

"Ben-jo? How 'bout using one of the bathrooms up-stairs?"

"I don't got time, Uncle Ty. Puleeeeeease."

"All right. Let me unlock the door."

No, Sophie mouthed, but Tyler reassured her. "Stay behind the door," he whispered into her ear, reaching back to right her zipper.

While Sophie held her shoes clutched to her chest, Tyler opened the door. Ben shot past, followed by Cody, and both boys disappeared behind the privacy wall.

Sophie took advantage of the moment, slipped under Tyler's arm and out into the empty bedroom. He grabbed her hand before she moved more than a step away.

"We're not done here," he growled.

"We're done *here*," she answered, nodding toward the bathroom.

"Yeah, but we're not done."

A totally un-Sophie hoydenish smile curled her upper lip.

"I'm done," she said, and scurried away.

Vixen. Tyler shut the door, leaned back against it and closed his eyes. This was it. No more. He was herding everyone outta here and taking Sophie home. One way or another, they would finish this tonight.

At the sound of tiny whispers, he looked down. Ben and Cody stood side by side, Ben's darker head bent down to his fair-haired brother's. What were the rascals up to now? "Can I help you boys with something?"

Ben shot up straight, his green eyes wide. Cody covered his mouth with one hand. Tyler crossed his arms and put on a frown.

Finally, shuffling from one boot to another, Ben said, "You better hurry up and go, Uncle Ty."

"Go where, Ben-jo?"

Cody giggled. "To da poddy, Unca Ty."

Ben nodded, his face serious. "Momma says not to wait cuz it's bad for your tummy. I think you better go now."

Tyler took in the direction of both boys' gaze and realized they were eye level with his erection. Great.

"Thanks, boys." Tyler opened the bathroom door. "I'll do that."

Ben followed Cody out the door. "He probly wants to be private like Momma and Daddy."

"Dey ahways want pwivate," Cody added sagely.

Tyler closed the door and decided he'd just changed his mind about kids.

IT WASN'T LIKE HER to be this nervous, this antsy, this unsure of herself. But since Tyler Barnes had come into her life, Sophie hadn't been sure of much of anything, except that for every answer she came up with today, tomorrow would bring two questions. She was tired of the uncertainty.

After she'd left the party with Harley and the baby, she'd changed back into her Sophie clothes, needing to meet Tyler tonight on her own turf and her own terms. Harley had driven her home.

The party had been fun, the kiss she'd shared with Tyler in the bathroom the stuff of fantasies. But this was now and this was real and this was the beginning of her future.

Standing behind the love seat in the cabin's main room, wearing her blue jeans, her work boots and her scooped and scalloped long-sleeved white T-shirt, she surveyed the stage she'd set, one part of her listening for the bump and rattle of tires over the new bridge.

She looked out over the room, at the flickering contrasts of light and shadow thrown by the low-burning fire. At the row of emergency candles she'd set into jar lids and lined across the footlocker's brass edge.

At the tiny Christmas bush she'd uprooted from the edge of the creek, planted in a silver pail and decorated with long stalks of winter grass tied into bows.

The mattress still lay in front of the fireplace, the sheets sun-dried and fresh. Orange peels, cloves and cinnamon simmered in a pot on the stove. This night would be a celebration of discovery and it deserved a festive mood.

Because this was the first time she'd ever been in love.

The bridge beams bumped and so did her heart. An engine roared to match the rush of her blood. A door slammed and the sound punched her in the stomach. Footsteps pounded onto the porch and nailed her into place on the floor.

The door opened and there he stood, the wolf, the wild animal, the man. Tall and broad-shouldered, long-legged and strong. He'd come for what he wanted, to finish what they'd started, to stake his final claim.

Panic rolled through Sophie on a shiver, trailing tails of expectation, sensation and desire. It was time.

Tyler kicked the door closed, pulled the black beaver Stetson from his head and tossed it onto the kitchen table. When he started to shrug off his jacket, she interrupted.

"You might want to leave that on."

He shook his head. "We don't have time to take our time."

She twisted her hands at her waist, shoved them deep into her pockets. "Not even time for foreplay?"

His eyes heated. "What do you call what we just did in my bathroom?"

"That was over an hour ago."

"I know. I've counted every second since," he said, but kept the jacket on.

She gave a small, hesitant shrug, glanced toward the mattress then back to the impatience in his face. "Since the board is all that's left of the Scrabble game, I thought we could play cards. Maybe a game of...poker?"

He arched one brow, then the other and propped his hands at his waist. The tails of his coat flared behind him and he advanced, slowly shaking his head.

Oh, God, he was right, she thought, and stared at the row of candles, the flickering gold lights and reflective silver bases. She and Tyler had reached this point too often already. It was time to toss her plan, go with his and just do it.

But then she remembered the way he'd looked while playing Scrabble, the way he'd looked at her tonight when she'd walked into the room.

She wanted to take him to that edge again. To see on his face what she felt in his body and know that the feelings burning between them reached all the way to his soul.

Taking a deep breath, she looked at him then, caught a teasing hint of the big bad wolf in the smile that claimed both his eyes and his mouth. When he walked toward her, her breathing stopped, started again at the touch of his hand on her elbow.

He guided her to one side of the mattress, stepped over to the other and made himself comfortable. Sprawled out on one side, one elbow braced on the love seat, he picked up her deck of cards and shuffled them from hand to hand. "We need to establish the rules here."

Sophie crossed her ankles, folded her legs and sat. So far, so good. "The first one would be that you're the dealer?"

"If you insist," he said, and winked.

"And the second?" she asked, the butterflies floating through her stomach making it hard for her to catch a normal breath.

"The winner of each hand gets his or her pick of the loser's clothing."

She had on enough layers that she could live with since she didn't intend to lose more than one or two hands anyway. "All right? Any more rules?"

"Just one."

"Yes?"

"From here on out, neither of us is allowed to say the word stop."

At this point it was heaven to have that decision taken out of her hands. It gave her the freedom of...freedom, exploration. Especially since she knew if she told him to stop, he'd stop.

"Five card stud?"

"I thought you'd never ask," he said, and dealt the first hand.

She let him deal, because he was obviously going to anyway, and because her hands were shaking too badly to handle a deck of cards. Or even a measly hand of five, she realized ruefully as the cards Tyler dealt her ended up in her lap.

"Nervous?" he asked, his eyes alight with male pleasure.

"Just being my usual clumsy self."

"I don't think so, Sophie. I've seen you splice wires the size of filaments. There's not a clumsy bone in your body."

Well, he would know about that. "Ah, but wiring doesn't count. I can do that with my eyes closed."

"You can do this with your eyes closed, too."

How did he do it every time? How did he word his replies for the most effect. "That's not the kind of eyes closed that I meant."

"What did you mean?" he asked, carefully arranging the cards in his hand.

"Just that I can splice wire without thinking about it. It's second nature. This..."

"This you've already thought about or we wouldn't be here now. Am I right?"

He was right, she realized, and glanced at the fire. She'd thought about it and thought about it and thought about it. She was tired of thinking and beginning to wonder if they should just finish what they'd started in the bathroom.

Foreplay wasn't supposed to be this much work.

"Well?" Tyler asked, and she looked away from the fire and back to his face.

"You're right," she said, and held her breath, waiting for him to tug the cards from her hand and toss them into the fire.

But he said, "Great. Then let's play."

Okay. He wanted to play cards, she'd play cards. What she wouldn't do was remind herself that she'd gotten herself into this mess. She covertly studied the back of his hand and glanced at the faces of the ones she held.

And that's when she realized the first of her mistakes. Five card stud was a game of chance. She had to accept the hand she was dealt and live with the consequences—consequences that she knew in advance because *she* had marked the cards.

Her second mistake was letting Tyler deal, but that one didn't matter since she'd made a third mistake of failing to learn to cheat as a dealer.

Her biggest mistake of all, though, was thinking the cards mattered. Because they didn't. She was going to make love with Tyler no matter what, and her stomach knotted in anticipation.

She slowly lifted her gaze, took the pair of twos he'd placed on the mattress and added her pair of aces. "I'd like your jacket, please."

He shrugged out of his jacket, one corner of his mouth curved upward as he said, "My pleasure."

She was sure this was going to be *her* pleasure, but she'd let him play the gentleman.

Tyler shuffled again, dealt again and this time Sophie's hands didn't shake as much as they had the first round. She told herself this burst of confidence had nothing to do with the fact that she'd won game two.

Tyler frowned and laid down five cards with nothing in common before she laid down three of a kind.

"Belt, please."

He released his buckle and pulled the strip of leather through the loops. His eyes darkened as he rolled the belt in his palm. "I think I'll keep this handy just in case."

"Just in case what?" she asked.

"Just in case you keep winning."

"Very funny," she said, even as an illicit thrill tickled low and deep.

In the next two rounds she divested him of his boots. And while he dealt hand number five, grumbling under his breath, Sophie's imagination went wild.

If her luck continued, he was going to be naked, she was going to be fully clothed—a scenario she hadn't considered. One that would put him at her mercy. Ah, she thought, arranging her cards. Justice after all.

"What's the smile for?"

She looked up then. "Just thinking."

"About?"

"I think I like this game. You know, 'Eeny-meeny-miney-moe, which piece of clothing is next to go.'"

Tyler looked at his hand then back at her face. His expression settled into one of satisfaction and Sophie felt the first rush of expectant fear.

"Well, darlin'. Unless you can beat this, I have a feeling the choice will be mine," he said, and laid down four of a kind.

Sophie looked down at her puny pair of sevens. Rats. It was bound to happen. She placed her cards on the mattress, freeing her hands to work the laces of her boots. Or to remove her T-shirt at Tyler's command, she thought, feeling the flush rise.

She waited for him to choose, waited, meeting his bold gaze with a calm she didn't feel. He rubbed his chin as if pondering a decision of greater importance than her sanity.

And then he finally said, "I want your panties."

Her heart jumped. "My panties?"

"Yeah, darlin'. Your panties."

"But that means..."

"It means I've made good use of the rules."

Rules to which she'd agreed. He was asking for the item of clothing he wanted. And she had to do the honorable, if not downright erotic, thing of stripping while he watched.

Removing clothing wasn't a big deal, she told herself, reaching for the laces on her right boot. She took them off every day. Often more than once. But she did it in private.

Though the intimate space humming with life between the four walls of this room wasn't exactly a stadium, she wasn't used to an audience. Not an audience whose green eyes flickered with the lights from the fire and brighter lights from deep within. Whose chest rose and fell with ragged breaths she could hear above the pop and sputter of dry fire.

She tossed the first boot behind her, reached for the laces of the second, licked at her lips, dabbed at the moisture beaded above and decided that the breathing she heard was her own. It filled her ears until all she could hear was the air moving in and out of her lungs, her heart pumping a rush of blood through her veins.

The second boot joined the first. And she reached for her socks, glad they were clean and glad that Harley had talked her into a quick pedicure. The pale pink polish glittered, but Tyler couldn't see it because he was watching her face.

She didn't have to look at him to know the direction of his gaze, she could feel it as surely as she'd felt his fingertips in his bathroom tonight. As surely as she'd be feeling them again.

Oh, God, she thought, moving her hands to her zipper. She got to her knees, tugged down the denim, then sat and slowly pulled each leg free.

Her fingers were cold and shaking and Tyler was just sitting there, patiently waiting, quietly waiting, his elbows propped behind him on the love seat, his legs stretched out long.

She turned her back to him, stared into the fire, watched the tongues of flame lick at the wood and remembered his touch. Her body warmed from the inside out, the temperature of her flesh increased by degrees as she closed her eyes and imagined. Hooked her thumbs in the elastic waist of her panties and pretended. Tugged the material down her thighs and made believe.

Then she turned to the side, leaned on one hip and

kicked the material free. With Tyler looking on, she folded the panties once, twice and handed them over.

He took them, held them, folded his hand around them, but his eyes never left hers, never traveled down her naked body, never looked at the scrap of material he held in his hand.

The moment stretched as did the silence and the endless beating of her heart. She sat with her legs folded to one side, her hands on the mattress at her hips and waited for Tyler to make his move, the heat of the fire toasting her back.

Her fingers cramped and the sheet beneath her palms grew damp. Her legs ached from holding them tight and gathered to her body. The pulse throbbing through her body settled as an ache that only he could fill.

Finally he looked at his hand, at her panties. Reaching out, he laid them on the footlocker beneath the Christmas tree then got to his knees, tugged his shirt from his pants and popped the row of snaps.

"This is your full house to my three of a kind," he said, and tossed his shirt behind him, baring his chest, the long expanse of skin dusted with hair, the ridge of muscles low on his abdomen.

"This is your flush to my straight," he said, and reached for his button fly. He released each copper button, slipped the jeans over his lean hips and down his cowboy-strong legs.

Kneeling in front of her in Christmas-red boxers, he lifted the hem of her shirt and tugged up. She raised her arms and, feeling no shame, no embarrassment, no uncertainty of any kind, she let him strip her naked.

"This is my royal flush to your two pairs," he said,

and lowered them both to the mattress. His elbows bracketed her shoulders, his hands cupped her head.

The first slow press of his chest to her breasts was bliss. She wrapped her arms around his waist and held him tight, skimmed her hands over his boxers to the backs of his hair-dusted legs. She wiggled, fitting her body to his, allowing his silk-covered erection to settle and lay heavy between her thighs.

She looked up into his eyes and, when she saw what she knew to be love, she smiled. He smiled back and began. He lowered his mouth to hers, tasted her, taught her his ways, let her take her fill.

Her hands roamed over smooth skin, muscles, counted the vertebrae down his spine to the small of his back, skimmed along the waistband of his boxers.

She pulled her mouth away, looked into his eyes and said, "There's still one hand left to play."

"This one's your call," he said.

Her body couldn't wait any longer. Neither could her soul. "Then this is the end of the game," she said, and slid his boxers over his hips.

He rolled to the side, kicked them free. When he returned, she welcomed the beautiful feel of his aroused body between her legs.

He sprinkled light kisses along her jaw, her cheek, the tip of her nose. While one hand cradled her head, the other ran the length of her body, over a breast, her belly, then traveled lower to test her readiness.

She was ready and he smiled.

He eased up to his knees and she watched, fascinated, as he took care of protection. His body was beautiful, rigid and ready with a dense weight shadowed beneath. She wanted him. Oh, how she wanted him. She reached up and let him know, pulling him down until he covered her, wrapping her legs around his hips.

He slid home and she arched upward, too ready for him to take the time this first coming together deserved. She urged him to move with her palms, digging her fingers deep, begging him to fill her again and again. But he stopped, suspending the moment and making her cry out.

"Please, Tyler. Please."

"In a minute, darlin'," he said, his breathing as harsh as hers, the sweat from his chest coating her body, the hardness of his stomach pressing deep. "I want you to feel something."

He leaned to the side, took her hand and cupped her fingers beneath the base of his sex. Placing his fingers above, he entwined their hands around the intimacy of their bodies. Then he began to move.

Braced up on one elbow, he slid his body in and out of hers, between the circle of their hands, making them one in ways she'd never dreamed of. Through it all, his eyes never left her face.

And when every breath she took caught, when she could no longer remain still, when her fingers slipped from their hot wet skin, he finally released her hand.

"Wrap your legs around me, darlin', and hold on tight."

She did, crying out as the motion of his body pulled her toward her release. She came back swiftly, opened her eyes to find his gaze on her face, his mouth taut, the veins in his neck lit in sharp relief by the light from the fire.

He was waiting for her to finish, holding his body in check, giving to her while denying himself. She couldn't have loved him more. "I love you, Tyler."

"Ah, Sophie," he groaned as his body shuddered and came to rest in her arms.

She held him there, wrapped close to her heart. And slowly, with the sweet farewell of a clearing mist, the feeling of homesickness faded to be replaced with a sense of coming home.

11

SOPHIE WOKE ALONE the next morning. Except she was sure morning had come and gone hours ago. She wasn't surprised to find that Tyler had already left. He'd told her that he had to make early rounds. She just hoped he functioned better than she did on only an hour of sleep.

She really needed to get up. And she would. She really would. In another minute or two.

She hadn't slept much during the night—an hour here, thirty minutes there—because every time Tyler reached for her she'd willingly turned and gone to him. The night before hadn't provided much rest, either, what with lying on that vinyl couch in the clinic and listening for sounds from the treatment room.

So much had happened the last two days that she'd barely found time to draw a breath. Her body had obviously picked the wee hours of this morning to shut down and to stay shut down until way past sunrise.

Pulling the quilt to her chin, she scooted toward Tyler's half of her side of the mattress, searching for the heat from his body. The sheets were toasty but she knew instinctively the temperature was due to the fire. It wasn't the same warmth she'd lain beneath so many times during the night.

Still, she stayed, enjoying the way his scent lingered, almost as if he'd left it for her as a gift, a reminder of what they'd created and a promise that he'd be there for her always. She had no doubt he'd live up to his word, even a word he hadn't spoken because that was the type of man he was.

One who loved his family, took care of his own. One who would let nothing keep him from a daughter who needed him. Especially not for twenty-one years.

Sophie blew out a huff of breath and ran both hands through her hair, shoving away the segue to that thought. She'd think of her father later. For now she only had time for Tyler.

She scrunched around on the mattress and sat up, pulling her knees to her chest. The cold hit her bare back and bare bottom. Shivering, she wrapped herself in the quilt literally from head to toe. The chill gradually waned, a wake-up yawn followed. It was time to get going and figure out where she went from here.

No, that wasn't quite true, she thought, stacking both pillows between her back and the love seat and staring into the flames of the fire Tyler had banked before leaving. She knew exactly where she wanted to go, what she wanted to do.

She wanted to travel her life with Tyler, to celebrate each moment with his generous gifts, to thank him for loving her. To love him in return.

The stability, the security, the friendship and respect. The feeling of family and belonging. Everything she'd been searching for throughout her life had been handed to her in a heartbreakingly sweet package.

And she wanted to make him a home, even if the concept was as alien to her as it was intrinsic to Tyler. He'd never had to put much effort into keeping a family together—at least until now, she thought and smiled to herself.

Now the real work began. All she knew was solitude, T-shirts, work boots and blue jeans. Home cooking had only recently become a part of her vocabulary. She didn't know a thing about being a wife or a mother. But she could do anything she set her mind to. Especially now that she'd experienced that "willing" part. Talk about incentive. And lessons learned.

She shook her head at the ironic state of rights and wrongs. Her judgment of passion as a destructive force had been so incredibly accurate. It had destroyed her mother, driven away her father, ruined her younger years and tainted her outlook on the relationships between men and women.

But that's because the passion she had witnessed involved bodies and nothing more. Tyler had taught her a new definition, a passion that transcended mere flesh and encompassed the soul.

And what she felt for him. Oh, what she felt for him. That sense of completeness came from a place deep within. A place she'd never known to look for, had never had reason to look for. A place that was waiting to be explored.

It was a thing of life mates and destinies and if she got any more poetic she was going to cry.

She didn't have time to cry. There were too many things she needed to settle. But she needed a truck to get started.

She had no idea when Tyler would return and quite frankly she didn't have the patience to wait to find out.

Camelot wasn't that far away and was probably her best bet for securing temporary wheels.

After a longer than planned hot shower and the realization that not all of her muscles were as toned as she'd thought, Sophie pulled on her T-shirt and jeans and a black and yellow plaid flannel shirt.

She added her denim jacket and boots, leaving Tyler a note that said, "I'll be back as soon as I can. Take good care of my dog. And extra good care of yourself." She left the note on her pillow, then set off on foot for the five mile trek down the county highway to Camelot's main gate.

By the time she reached the ranch an hour later it was nearly noon. She heard workday sounds coming from the barnyard and pastures. Shouted orders. Machinery. Dogs barking. The low of cattle.

She walked around the house to the screened-in back porch, climbed the steps to the sound of a child's laughter. And Harley's. It was a sound of happiness, pleasure, one that had been absent in the home she'd grown up in. One she wanted to make a part of her new life.

Feeling the smile spread over her face, she reached up and knocked on the back door.

"In here," Harley called, and Sophie stepped into the room.

"Am I disturbing you?"

"Of course not. C'mon in. Sit down." Wearing a huge navy sweatshirt and her hair pulled back in a ponytail, Harley sat on the far side of the long kitchen table. Cody sat to her left, propped up on a booster seat. "Have you had lunch?"

Shaking her head, Sophie pulled out a chair across

from the pair. "I haven't even had breakfast. I'm still recovering from the barbecue last night."

"Tell me about it." Harley puffed out her cheeks. "I cannot believe how much I ate. But Cody here of the bottomless stomach was ready for lunch. So, since Dani's sleeping, we decided to play alphabet soup."

Sophie noticed the wad of soup-stained paper towels in the center of the table and the tiny pasta letters lined up on a carrot stick on Cody's plate. A learning lunch. She never would have imagined.

"Did Tyler drop you off so I could keep an eye on you?" Harley asked.

Sophie appreciated the way Harley so casually asked the question. She had to know Tyler hadn't returned to Camelot last night, that he'd stayed at the cabin. But she didn't seem anything but accepting.

And why wouldn't she be? She'd told Sophie exactly how it was to be loved by and love a Barnes man. Sophie relaxed her clenched fists, and pulled her hands from the deep pockets in her jacket. "No...he left early this morning. I walked over."

Harley blinked once. "You walked over?"

"It's only about five miles."

"Yeah. Five miles down the county highway. It's at least another two from the main gate to the house. Is everything okay?"

Sophie shrugged. "Yeah. I just felt like a walk. And it really didn't seem that far."

"Maybe not to your twenty-something-year-old legs."

A smile pulled at Sophie's lips. "And how many

times a day do you go up and down that flight of stairs?''

Harley glanced over her shoulder to the staircase then back at Sophie. "About seven miles worth."

"Momma. Can I be scuzed now?"

Harley looked over and ruffled Cody's hair. "Are you full?"

He nodded, his bottom lip solemn.

"Too full to eat that last red car?" Harley asked, pointing to the letters on the carrot.

Cody giggled. "My tummy doesn't have room for a car."

"All right, sweetie." Harley cleaned his mouth with a paper towel. "You run upstairs and pick out a book for quiet time."

Cody scrambled down out of the chair and stopped at the bottom of the staircase. "Can Sophie come, too?"

"Sure she can, but she and I have some grown-up talk to do first, okay?"

Cody rolled his eyes. "Aways gwown-up talk," he said, and stomped his little boots up the stairs.

"He's really cute," Sophie said, wondering what Tyler's children would look like.

"He's really cranky," Harley replied, gathering the soiled towels into a single heap. "I don't blame him, though. He gets lonely during the day while Austin and Ben are at school, especially now that I'm tied up with Dani. The days Gardner spends in the Rover instead of on horseback, he's been good to let Cody tag along."

"Today wasn't one of those days, I guess."

"Ah, but it was and that's why he's especially cross." Harley got to her feet, her chair legs scraping over the tiled floor. She carried Cody's near-empty bowl to the sink. "He's getting over an ear infection and too much fresh air yesterday sent him to bed with an earache. I'm determined to keep him inside today."

"Even if it kills him?"

"Even if it kills *me*." She tossed the towels in the garbage and wiped down the table with a rag. "I promised him we'd have an extra story time."

"Then I should go and let you get to him." Sophie started to rise, but Harley waved her back down.

"Not until you tell me what was worth walking seven miles for."

Good point. "I really came by to ask a favor."

Harley moved Cody's booster seat and plopped down in his chair. She pulled her knees to her chest, tucked the heels of her Keds close to her backside. "Anything. What do you need?"

Sophie looked down, ran her finger over a scar in the wooden table. "I need to borrow a truck. I have some loose ends I need to tie up..."

"And you're stranded here, aren't you?" Harley slapped her palm against the table. "I can't believe Tyler didn't think of that and lend you one of the trucks around here."

"It really wasn't much of an issue before today. I mean, up until yesterday I had access to a crew truck."

"Well, you're more than welcome to anything we have around here."

"I may be gone a few days."

One of Harley's neat brows arched then lowered. "Are you leaving?"

"No. I mean, I'll be back." She traced the scar on the

table again. And again. "Cowboy, my dog, still isn't totally healed. And then there's...Tyler." Sophie moved her hands back to her jacket pockets and slowly raised her gaze.

Harley had the sweetest smile on her face. A big sister type of smile. Or a best friend type of smile. And Sophie found it hard not to cry.

Her arms wrapped around her knees, her head cocked to one side, Harley said, "You know, you are so perfect for him."

Sophie wanted so badly to believe that was true. To believe that beyond his declarations and demonstrations of love, that deep down she met his needs the way he so completely met hers.

"I think he's pretty perfect all by himself," she said.

"Well, yes, that he is. But then, he *is* a Barnes." Harley grinned then grew sober. "The thing about Tyler is that as much as he needs someone to care for him, he needs someone to care for. The work he does with the animals, the healing and caregiving, has helped him channel those feelings. But it's not enough anymore."

Sophie hated to sound desperate to know, but...well, she was desperate to know. "Can you, I mean, will you..."

"Tell you why? I'll do my best," Harley said. Then added, "You have to understand that when I married Gardner, Tyler was already eighteen and on his way to college. But it hasn't been hard to figure out where Tyler comes from after piecing together Gardner's stories. He was always more a parent than a brother to Tyler, even before their mother and father died."

"Is that when Jud came to live with them? After their parents died?" Sophie asked.

Harley nodded. "Tyler was ten. Gardner, twenty-two. Gardner and Jud worked the ranch and Tyler did what he could between regular chores and school. That kind of exhaustion doesn't leave much energy to expend on nurturing a family.

"Gardner was older. He'd convinced himself that he didn't need anyone. He blamed his determination to remain uninvolved on the demands of the ranch, when it was really the only way he knew to keep from making a mistake," Harley said with the certainty of a woman who knew her man.

"I think that's what's called self-preservation," Sophie said with equal conviction.

Harley unfolded from the chair and sat forward, squeezing Sophie's hand in a silent gesture of understanding. "Self-preservation. Exactly. But, Tyler...he was just a boy when his parents died. His needs were huge. And Gardner and Jud could only do so much."

"And so he turned to the animals?"

Nodding, Harley got to her feet. She filled a teakettle with water and set it on the stove. "Do you want a cup of tea? Or coffee?"

"Tea would be nice. Thank you."

"You're quite welcome," Harley said, grabbing two mugs, cream and sugar, and a tin of aromatic tea bags. She settled back into her chair, chose her tea and continued her story. "I don't know if Tyler expected to come home from school and pick up where he'd left off, but I do know that he's not as happy here as he was ten years ago. At least he wasn't until you came along." When the kettle whistled, she hopped up and poured. "And that just proves my theory."

"Which is?" Sophie asked, warming her palms on the sides of her cup.

"That the focus he's missing is the love of a good woman. Oh, I'm sure if he heard my analysis he'd call it bunk, but I doubt if he could come up with a better one." She pointed a finger in Sophie's direction. "And that's because there's not a rational explanation for the whys of what goes on between a man and a woman."

Wasn't that exactly what Tyler had said? Sophie stared into the transparent liquid, searching for an equal clarity of mind. "His intensity frightens me at times. Or overwhelms me, I guess I should say. I haven't had any experience with love to speak of. I'm afraid I won't be able to love him back the way he deserves."

"Oh, sure you will, honey. Lovin's an easy thing to do."

"I don't want to disappoint him," Sophie said, feeling a rush of emotion well in her eyes.

"At this point, the only way you can disappoint him is by leaving and not coming back. You are coming back?"

Sipping her tea, Sophie nodded.

"All right, then." Harley got to her feet. "Let's go find you a set of wheels."

They headed out the back door and were halfway down the steps when Gardner pulled his Range Rover to a stop. He climbed down and walked in their direction, meeting them at the foot of the stairs.

"Afternoon, wife," he said, giving Harley a quick kiss

before glancing in Sophie's direction. "Afternoon, Sophie. I see you managed to escape my brother long enough to pay us a visit."

Sophie adored the relationship Gardner shared with Harley and was quite sure it showed in the smile on her face. "He's out making rounds with Doc Harmon."

"Did he drop you off here for safekeeping?"

Harley laughed before Sophie could say a word. "That's exactly what I asked her. But Tyler doesn't know she's here. She walked over."

"She's young. She can do that sort of thing," Gardner said to Harley. Then, to Sophie, "Did you want a lift back? Or do you need to make a grocery run into town? I'd be glad to give you a ride."

"I think she has a few more errands in mind than she can accomplish in Brodie, Gardner," Harley said from her husband's side, sending a wink at Sophie. "I told her we'd lend her a truck. One we won't be needing for a day or two."

Gardner frowned. "You're not leaving town, are you?"

"Only long enough to take care of a few things. Oh, and here's the DayLine number in Houston if Tyler needs to get in touch with me about Cowboy...or anything," she said, pulling a business card from her pocket.

Harley took the card from her hand. "You know Tyler's going to freak when he comes home to find you gone."

"I know. But I have to do it this way..."

"Or else you might not do it at all," Harley finished

for her, and Sophie nodded, appreciating this woman's understanding.

Making a sweeping glance of the yard, Gardner seemed oblivious to their small female interchange. "I don't think we'll have a bit of trouble fixing you up with a truck. Either the blue pickup over there—" he pointed toward the vehicles parked between the bunkhouse and the barn "—or the Jeep beside it would be the best. Depends on whether or not you need the cargo area."

"The Jeep will be fine. I don't need a lot of room."

"Then I'll go get the keys," Harley said, and turned to go.

"Uh, Harley. I'll get the keys." Gardner pointed toward the second-story window where Cody's little face was pressed to the glass.

"Oh, good grief," Harley exclaimed as Gardner headed inside. "I'd better get upstairs before we find out they were kidding when they called it safety glass." She stepped forward and gave Sophie a hug. "You take care, okay? And I'll see you soon?"

Sophie nodded, adding another notch of comfort to the decision she'd come to. "Tell Cody I'll read him a story when I get back."

"I'll do that," Harley said with a wave as she walked into the house.

Gardner appeared a moment later and Sophie fell into step beside him as he headed toward the Jeep. "Tyler took this thing out across the pasture after an injured calf not too long back, but I think we got it all cleaned up."

While Gardner checked the fluid levels under the Jeep's hood, Sophie stood back and took in the vastness and stark beauty of her surroundings. When Tyler had talked about the lure of home, the dream of setting up his practice, he'd talked mostly of the people, his extended family.

He hadn't talked much about the land, or his need to return to this piece of God's earth he called home. But she knew that had to be a part of his decision. Even she could feel the pull of the untamed skies, the sense of forever in the land. For the first time in all her travels, she knew she'd found a place she could stay. A reason to stay. And a man to make her happy.

The Jeep hood slammed and Gardner walked toward her, wiping his hands on a rag. "You know, Sophie. Things with you and Tyler are none of my business, but I've gotta say I'm glad you came along when you did."

"Why?" she asked. "Am I keeping him out of your hair?"

"Well, there is that." Gardner grinned. "But more than that, you're keeping him happy. I'm grateful." He held the key ring on one finger. "She's all yours."

Sophie took the keys and climbed into the Jeep. "Thanks. For everything."

He shrugged. "I thought you might like to know. I mean, if it was Harley, she'd want to know."

"You figured that out about her, huh?"

"She took my failure-to-communicate gene and beat me with it, up one side and down the other. And that was *before* we were married."

That must be the mistake Tyler had mentioned. Sophie started the Jeep. "I haven't run into that problem yet. If I do, I'll keep Harley's solution in mind. Thanks again. Tell Harley I'll see her soon."

Anxious to stop by the clinic and check on Cowboy before hitting the road, she put the Jeep in gear, started forward then stopped. "And tell Tyler..."

"Tell Tyler what?"

She smiled to herself. "Tell Tyler that I changed my mind. The game's not over."

12

"WHAT DO YOU MEAN you loaned her a Jeep?" Tyler asked, slamming the door of his truck.

Gardner parked his hands on his hips. "She asked for a vehicle and I gave her one."

"You gave her one?"

"To use, Tyler. To use."

"When did she say she'll be back?"

"A couple of days at the most."

"A couple of days?" It didn't matter that he told himself to calm down. It wasn't happening. "Where did she go?"

"I didn't ask."

"You didn't ask?"

Gardner cupped his hand to his ear. "Is there an echo out here or is it just me?"

Tyler slammed a fist into the shiny red hood. "How could you not ask?"

"She told Harley she had a few things to take care of," Gardner said, looking from the fist-size dent to Tyler's face. "I don't think she's used to asking for permission to take care of her personal business."

"Yeah, but I don't even know where she is," Tyler grumbled, kicking his heels at the packed earth as he walked around to the front of his truck.

Gardner followed. "She left Harley a number in

Houston. In case of an emergency, they'll contact her. Look, Tyler. You've picked yourself a strong-willed woman. Don't think you're gonna change that about her."

"I don't want to change that about her. I don't want to change *anything* about her," he added more for his own benefit than Gardner's.

"Then make sure you can deal with it before you make a huge mistake and the both of you end up miserable."

"It's not a mistake." He leaned his backside against the bumper of his truck, braced his hands on his thighs and hung his head. "It's not a mistake."

"You don't trust her?"

"Yes, I trust her."

"Then give her the time she needs. And if she doesn't come back..."

"She'll come back. I have her dog, remember?" That thought of Cowboy was all that kept him from going after her.

"Then make sure that's not all she comes back for. That she comes back for the right reason."

"That's not what I'm worried about. I'm afraid that when she gets here, she'll leave again. For the wrong reasons." He waited a minute and, when Gardner didn't say anything more, content to let him stew, Tyler added, "She thinks she's going to ruin my life."

"From what I've seen, your life could use a good ruining."

Tyler glared up at his brother. "Very funny."

"Hell, Tyler. Ever since you've come home, something's been wrong. I've noticed it. Harley's noticed it.

And it looks like it took Sophie to set it right. Either she shook up what needed shaking. Or she fixed whatever wasn't sitting right. It's more than obvious that she's good for you. But you've got to consider that you might not be the best thing for her."

Tyler didn't want to consider that at all. But he had to. There was a very good chance that what he'd shared with Sophie had brought her to a reckoning with herself and nothing more. That even though she'd shown him with her body and told him with the words that she loved him, that what she felt was gratitude, and that she'd said the words as a thank-you.

He didn't want a thank-you. He wanted Sophie, body and soul.

The ring of the dinner bell interrupted.

"You comin' in?" Gardner asked.

"I'll be in later." He pushed off the truck, headed toward the barn. Gardner stepped in front of him and Tyler looked up.

"If you want to talk about it, I'll do what I can to help."

"Thanks, but I think I'm gonna hafta handle this one on my own."

"You're probably right. I doubt I'd be much help anyway. The only thing I know about women is what I know about Harley. And I have a feeling she and Sophie are one of a kind." He started toward the house then stopped. "That reminds me. She told me to tell you that she'd changed her mind and the game's not over, whatever that means."

That brought a smile to Tyler's mouth. A small lift to his spirits. "Thanks."

He made his way to the barn, not even bothering to convince himself he was headed there for any reason other than the one that had brought him there time and again through the years. The cool darkness soothed him and he walked deeper into the shadows.

He'd always been able to think better in here. To find answers he hadn't managed to find anywhere else. As if in immersing himself in nature, the smells of earth and animals, the aura of what it took to survive, he was grounding himself in reality, what mattered, what was important.

What was important was Sophie. And facing the possibility that he wasn't what was best for her.

Gripping the top slat of a stall, he swung the door toward him and back, listening to the squeak of hinges and the creak of wood. Outside, ol' Pete and the other hands cut a path across the yard on their way to the house to be spoiled by another of Harley's incredible meals.

Tyler caught snatches of their conversation, bits about fences and feedings, a hearty thanks for the mild winter and talk of the spring calving to come.

It was the conversation of a family. A group of individuals with a common goal, a shared love for their work, a respectful appreciation of one another as members of a team.

Sophie belonged here more than she belonged on the road, living her life from a duffel bag, denying herself the dream of a degree, searching for her idea of a family instead of stopping to make one of her own.

No one could be better for her than he was. That was a fact and he refused to believe otherwise. He knew her, had shared her dreams and desires as intimately as he'd shared her body. And that last time, when she cried out that she'd need him forever, he was sure he'd convinced her to stay.

And who's to say that he hadn't? The game wasn't over. That's what she'd said. And that meant she'd only left long enough to settle business that needed settling. He had to believe that. Until he knew differently, he *would* believe that.

HE WAS STILL BELIEVING it five endlessly long nights later when he said good-night to Cowboy, shut off the lights in Doc Harmon's clinic and headed for his truck. It had been a hell of a day between the vaccination clinic and Stick Nichols's new colt tangling himself up in a coil of barbed wire.

Tyler was ready to inhale his dinner on his way to bed. Who cared if he smelled like a cross between sour laundry and a chemical spill? Harley cared. He grumbled to himself. She wouldn't feed him if he came into her kitchen without stopping for a shower to wash off the stink.

His fate was sealed. It was a shower or starvation. But if he walked into a house that smelled of anything close to meat and potatoes, he figured he could find the energy to climb the stairs to the bathroom.

The minute he opened his truck door, however, he forgot about his stomach because lying on his seat was a brand new Scrabble game tied up with a big red bow. He closed his eyes, opened them. The game was still there.

He moved it onto the dashboard where he could keep

an eye on it and climbed into the driver's seat. As he backed out of the lot, the truck's side mirror shot back a reflection of the grinningest damned fool he'd ever seen.

Wide awake now, he gunned the engine, spun through the gravel parking lot and burned rubber out onto the county highway. By the time he reached Camelot, he was running on adrenaline.

He fishtailed the truck into the yard, threw the gearshift into Neutral and set the brake. Halfway up the back stairs, he realized the truck was still running. He ran back to cut the engine only to find he'd locked the door.

If he kept this up, he'd never make it to Sophie. He jogged back toward the house, took the back stairs in two steps and snagged his set of spare keys from the hook in the washroom. He started back outside then heard Gardner's voice in the kitchen.

"Gardner. Do me a favor, will ya?" he asked, entering the room.

Gardner looked up from the screen of his laptop computer. He pulled off his reading glasses and laid them on the invoices stacked on the kitchen table. He caught the keys when Tyler tossed them. "You want me to take your truck and leave?"

"No, but would you mind turning it off? I locked the keys inside," he said, popping open the snaps on the front placket of his shirt.

Harley stepped off the bottom stair into the kitchen, a basket of dirty laundry in her hands. "I left you a plate of food in the fridge. I'll heat it up while you shower."

"I don't have time to eat," he said, jerking at his cuffs

and pulling off the shirt. He wadded it into a ball, hooped it into Harley's basket and headed up the stairs.

"Sophie's back."

BY THE TIME Tyler stopped off at the clinic to pick up Cowboy and got back on the road to Big O's, a cold mist had wrapped Brodie, Texas, in wintery fingers. The rain was soft, gentle. Nothing like the torrent the night he'd met Sophie.

He supposed it was fitting really. The way they'd come full circle. Back to the cabin in the rain.

One hand on Cowboy's head, the other on the wheel, he drove across the new bridge, diamond patterns of water suspended in the white beams thrown by his headlights. He frowned as he came closer; the cabin appeared to be dark. But then he picked up Gardner's Jeep parked off to one side and the flicker of what had to be a fire through the west window.

And then he saw Sophie on the porch, sitting with her back to the closed front door, her knees drawn to her chest, her jean jacket wrapped tight against the cold. Cutting off his headlights, Tyler used the yellow glow from his parking lights to guide the way.

He pulled his truck to a stop in front of the cabin steps, cut the lights and the engine, returning the night to darkness and a still silence broken only by the even breathing of the dog asleep on his seat.

He opened the door, climbed down and quickly eased it closed against the buzz of keys and the cab light. He'd let Cowboy sleep for the moment and take care of business first. Climbing the porch steps slowly, he ignored the splatter of cold water against his skin. He had eyes and senses only for Sophie.

"How was your trip?" he asked, leaning back against a porch post, blinking to adjust to the uncompromising blackness surrounding the cabin and the far-lying fields.

The rain eased a bit and a small break in the clouds followed. Moonlight spilled through, highlighting the curved red lines of his truck and catching the shine in Sophie's eyes.

"It was good," she said. "Too long, too lonely, but good."

He heard the exhaustion in her voice. "You accomplished what you needed to?" he asked, not wanting to pry but doing so anyway.

"I got quite a lot done as a matter of fact."

He straightened from the porch post and eased down into a crouch, putting himself at her eye level, trying to close the distance he suddenly felt.

But then he couldn't think of anything to say besides demanding to know where she'd gone, what she'd been doing, but most of all, what had brought her back.

He didn't want to make demands. This wasn't the time for demands. So he stared at the toe of one boot, wiped the beaded moisture from the black leather and let the tension mount.

"Tyler."

He looked up.

"You're getting wet."

He lifted a shoulder and shrugged. "I've been wet before."

"I know. I remember." She propped her chin in the vee of her updrawn knees. "I think you should move."

"Why?" he asked, feeling the smile pull at his mouth. "You afraid all this sugar's gonna melt right off of me?"

"No. Because I want you over here." She patted the porch next to her hip.

"Why?" he asked again, this time more somber because somber kept the hope at a level he could manage.

"Because I'm selfish and you're too far away."

He laughed, but stayed where he was. "You're about the least selfish person I know."

"I used to be." She stretched her legs out in front of her, crossed her ankles, tilted her toes this way and that. "But I've turned over a new leaf."

"Oh?" He kept his voice even while shifting his weight to the other foot.

"I quit my job."

His heart jumped at that. "What do you plan to do now?"

"If I'm very careful, I won't have to worry about money for a while."

"Are you going to go back to school?"

"I've thought about it. But I'm not sure it's what I want anymore. I don't think it was ever what I wanted. It was more what I felt would give me an advantage in finding my father. That's no reason to choose a career."

Tyler agreed, but there was more at stake here than her career. This was her life. "You're not going to stop looking for him, are you?"

She shook her head, the sprinkle of mist in her hair catching the light from the moon. "No, but I'm going to face the possibility that I may never find him. I'm not going to let it consume me like I have in the past. I'm not going to put my life on hold. A very wise young man taught me to live every moment. I've decided I can't afford to waste a single one."

She got to her feet slowly, and his eyes followed every move, the way her legs unfolded into forever, the way she held her chin at an angle that could have been arrogance but he knew to be conviction. She was beautiful and he couldn't look away. Neither could he move, even when she extended her hands.

"Why don't you come over here, very wise young man?"

He stood, keeping his fingers in his front pockets and the distance between them. "Sophie, I don't want to be the cause of you giving up your dream." That was a guilt he wouldn't be able to live with.

"Oh, Tyler, don't you see? You've given me my dream. You've taught me that I don't have to find the man who fathered me to have a family." She stepped forward, forced his hands from his pockets and held them tight. "For the first time in my life, I feel like I've truly come home."

Home. How long had he waited to hear her speak the word? He drew strength from the grip of her tiny fingers. "So you're going to stay?"

"I think I will." She let him go and turned toward the door, stopping with one hand on the latch. "And since I'm going to be here for more than likely the rest of my life, I may just learn to do a little home cooking."

"Oh, yeah?" The beginnings of that damned fool grin eased into place. "What else?"

"I may look into taking some vet tech classes. You

see, I know this veterinarian who could use some help from time to time.'' She pushed open the cabin door. The scent of coals and wood smoke drifted through the crack. "I'm cold. Let's go inside.''

He shook his head, looked out into the inky blackness and then back. He still wasn't ready. He still needed to know.

"What is it, Tyler?'' she asked softly.

He let her voice settle around him, soothe him. Then he spoke. "Before I walk inside that cabin with you I need the answer to a question. You told me why you left. But why did you come back?''

"You have to ask?''

He nodded.

"Then I'll tell you. I came back for my dog. For Harley and Gardner, who I consider two of my first real friends. For the wide-open spaces that give me room to breathe and more room to think than I'll ever need. Those are the reasons I came back, Tyler. But they're not the reasons I'm staying.

"I'm staying because I've found a man who makes me happy. Who thinks there's hope for me in spite of my hardheadedness and who wants me despite the fact that I don't have a clue about home and family.'' A tender smile turned up the corners of her mouth. Her lashes dampened as her eyes grew dreamy with tears. "I'm staying because I'm in love with you.''

He closed his eyes, feeling the storm of fear and denial subside, and drew the first full breath he'd drawn in five days. He walked closer to the door, measuring each step, watching Sophie's smile widen, her eyes grow impish and round.

"I hope you're sure about this, Sophie North."

"Of course I'm sure. Besides, it fits in so beautifully with the last of my plans."

"Which is?"

"To be engaged by the end of next year."

He arched a brow. "Oh, yeah?"

"Yeah. What do you have to say about that?" she asked, growing too cocky for her own good.

He was gonna love loving her. "Make that married by the end of this year and you're on."

"But it's almost Christmas."

"And I can't think of any gift I'd rather have than a wife."

"Not even that Scrabble game I left in your truck?"

"Aw, hell. Hold on a minute. I have a gift for you, too." He returned to his truck, scooped Cowboy into his arms and carried him onto the porch.

"Oh, Tyler," Sophie exclaimed, dropping to her knees and wrapping her arms gently around the dog. Cowboy licked at her cheek, glancing up at Tyler with a huge thank-you on his canine face while Sophie fawned and cooed.

Finally Sophie looked up, her eyes teary, but her smile the stuff of pure joy. "It's okay for him to come home?"

"Since he has a really good in with a vet, it should be fine," Tyler said, pushing open the door. "Let's get him inside."

Sophie followed the dog as he gingerly made his way to the hearth. Once there, he curled up as best he could onto the quilt that lay at the foot of the bed.

Sophie knelt beside him, stroking her hand over his

head, scratching his ears, speaking low words that only the dog could hear. Finally she realized Tyler still stood outside.

She got to her feet and went to him. "Aren't you coming in?"

He looked down at the green-eyed blond pixie who'd changed his life. "You know once I cross this threshold it's forever."

"I wouldn't have it any other way," Sophie said, and pulled him through the door, into her heart and into their home.

HARLEQUIN® Temptation.

'Twas the Night of Her Wedding...

And Belle Farentino can't believe what she's done—married a stranger to gain her inheritance. But Cade McBride is better than a stranger—he's a sexy drifter whose love-'em-and-leave-'em attitude is legend. Belle is counting on that reputation to get Cade out of her life once the wedding is over. But after spending one incredible night in his arms, Belle is having second thoughts....

Enjoy #626 AFTER THE LOVING by Sandy Steen Available in March 1997 wherever Harlequin books are sold.

IT HAPPENED ONE NIGHT

Five sensuous stories from Temptation about heroes and heroines who share a single sizzling night of love.... And damn the consequences!

**Is it better to know who you *are*...or
who you are *not*?**

SECRET SINS

Twenty-seven years ago on a cold and snowy night in
Cleveland a traffic pileup leaves at least four people dead.
One little girl survives. Though she calls herself Liliana, she
is proven to be Jessica Marie Pazmany—and her parents are
among the dead. The toddler is soon adopted and becomes
Jessica Marie Zajak.

Now her well-adjusted life quickly comes to a halt when
it is discovered that the little girl in the accident could not
possibly have been Jessica Marie Pazmany—because *she* died
seven months *before* the car crash. So who is Jessica? Who
was Liliana?

The next bestseller by internationally celebrated author

JASMINE CRESSWELL

Available in February 1997 at your favorite retail outlet.

 MIRA **The brightest star in women's fiction**

MJCSS

Look us up on-line at: http://www.romance.net

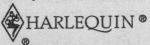

You are cordially invited to a

HOMETOWN REUNION

September 1996—August 1997

Bad boys, cowboys, babies. Feuding families,
arson, mistaken identity, a mom on the run...
Where can you find romance and adventure?
Tyler, Wisconsin, that's where!

So join us in this not-so-sleepy little town and
experience the love, the laughter and the
tears of those who call it home.

WELCOME TO A
HOMETOWN REUNION

Gabe Atwood has no sooner rescued his wife,
Raine, from a burning building when there's
more talk of fires. Rumor has it that Clint
Stanford suspects Jon Weiss, the new kid at
school, of burning down the Ingallses' factory.
And that Marina, Jon's mother, has kindled a fire
in Clint that may be affecting his judgment. Don't
miss Kristine Rolofson's *A Touch of Texas,*
the seventh in a series you won't want to end....

Available in March 1997
at your favorite retail store.

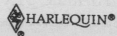

Heartbreak RANCH

Four generations of independent women...
Four heartwarming, romantic stories of the West...
Four incredible authors...

Fern Michaels
Jill Marie Landis
Dorsey Kelley
Chelley Kitzmiller

Saddle up with Heartbreak Ranch, an outstanding
Western collection that will take you on a whirlwind
trip through four generations and the exciting,
romantic adventures of four strong women who
have inherited the ranch from Bella Duprey,
famed Barbary Coast madam.

Available in March,
wherever Harlequin books are sold.

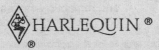

HARLEQUIN ®

®

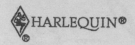

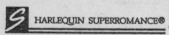
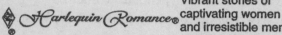